Charge It To The Game 2

FAMILY OR FOE

NAI

U.A.D PRESENTS

Stay Up to Date

To stay up to date on new releases, plus get information on contests, sneak peeks and more,

Click the link below...
https://mailchi.mp/6d21003686d1/subscribe

Soundtracks

Scan the QR Code below to listen to the Soundtracks/Singles of some of your favorite U.A.D titles:

Don't have Spotify or Apple Music?
No Sweat!
Visit your choice streaming platform and search URBAN AINT DEAD.

Currently on lock serving a bid?
JPay, iHeartRadio, WHATEVER!
We got you covered.
Simply log into your facility's kiosk or tablet, go to music and search
URBAN AINT DEAD.

U.A.D PRESENTS

Like & Follow us on social media:

FB - URBAN AINT DEAD

IG: @uadpresents

Tik Tok - @uadpresents

Submission Guidelines

Submit the first three chapters of your completed manuscript to urbanaintdead@gmail.com, subject line: Your book's title. The manuscript must be in a .doc file and sent as an attachment. The document should be in Times New Roman, double-spaced, and in size 12 font. Also, provide your synopsis and full contact information. If sending multiple submissions, they must each be in a separate email. Have a story but no way to submit it electronically? You can still submit to URBAN AINT DEAD. Send in the first three chapters, written or typed, of your completed manuscript to:

URBAN AINT DEAD
P.O Box 448
Maybrook, NY 12543

DO NOT send original manuscript. Must be a duplicate.
Provide your synopsis and a cover letter containing your full contact information.
Thanks for considering URBAN AINT DEAD.

Acknowledgments

And here we are again & I must say it feels DAMN GOOD! Let me tell you, this book took me through it so the only people I wanna thank is Janai, Nai, and Authoress Nai, LOL. Shoutout to The Hood Lover's Society!!! Y'all been on my neck about this part two and have kept me motivated. The writing process this go round has been unlike any other and y'all waited patiently. I swear we going up from here. That said, let's not prolong this thang any longer. IT'S A REAL B*TCH PARTY... LET'S GET INTO SOME GANGSTA SH*T, SHALL WE....

Chapter One

SANTANA

I watched Mahogany walk down the steps, hop in her car, and peel out of the driveway. Our brief interaction only confirmed that what I'd heard about her in the streets was definitely true. It was clear from the way that she'd pulled up that she wasn't stuntin' my ass or any thought of us working on our brother/sister bond. Hell, she wasn't even tryna claim a nigga as her blood. Talkin' bout some, she don't know me and I don't know her.

Granted, I'd been gone for a while, but it would never change the fact that we were family. To add insult to injury, that whole going through a preliminary screening as if I was some corner boy was bullshit. I was a fuckin' boss too, wasn't no mistaking that. Before she had even thought about stepping into the league, I had been up to bat plenty of times. Baby sis was cocky as hell and she had that honestly considering who she was raised by. She was Coolie through and through but carried herself much like our mama, who was a gangsta in her own right.

My vibrating phone snapped me from my thoughts, and I pulled it from my pocket. It was my pops calling. Checking over my shoulder to ensure that there were no extra ears in the vicinity, I stepped outside to take the call.

"What you on, pops?"

"Shit, cruisin' the city. How's the East Coast treating you so far, were you received with open arms?" I'd told him about my trip and the plans I intended to put in motion as far as The Table was concerned. He was all for it and had even given me a few tips as to how I could finesse the situation to come out on top.

"I only been here two days and I must say its been interesting to say the least."

"Oh, yeah? How so? Ay, walk or get run the fuck over!" I heard him bark at someone followed by an exaggerated beep of his car's horn.

"Man, you hell on that road," I chuckled. "You need to chill with that or stay from behind the wheel."

"Nah, these motherfuckin' pedestrians need to stop actin' like I drive on they time. This Chevy got a mind of her own. Fuck around and slide a motherfucka under this bitch." Frustration was evident in his voice. "You caught up witcho sister yet?"

"Man, yeah. And she ain't fuckin' wit me at all. I'm definitely gonna have to move on her terms for a minute in order to gain her trust. She ain't budging right now."

"Well, son, you knew this shit wasn't gon' be no walk in the park. Don't let it deter you from your ultimate goal, though. Remember, she's still a woman at the end of the day. Tap into her emotions, that's how you get to a woman."

"Coming from a nigga who ain't got a woman," I joked.

"Shiidd, you got plenty of step mamas, lil' nigga." We laughed.

"I hear you, but I can tell you now that Mahogany has been groomed well. She ain't giving out no breaks."

"Yeah, she sounds like ya mama. Speaking of Antoinette, have you seen her? What she looking like nowadays?"

"I'm actually at her crib now. I need to get back inside before she come looking for me." I turned to make sure the door was still closed. "And my mama still beautiful. Watchu tryna get into though, pop?" I asked him.

"Shit. I'm just asking. You know I don't fuck with her and she ain't a fan of mine. I bet that nigga Coolie got her living lavish,

huh? Sucka ass nigga." The jealousy dripped from his words and I shook my head. I didn't know the full history between my Pops and Coolie and at my grown ass age, I didn't care to ask.

All I knew was that he didn't fuck with Coolie. The logical explanation I'd come up with in my head was that maybe Pops was still feeling a way about another man having raised me for the first eleven years of my life. Knowing him though, it had to be deeper than that.

"She's being taken care of," was the response I provided. My phone beeped, indicating another call. Seeing Razor's name on the screen, I cut the conversation with my pops short. **"Ay, Pop, lemme hit you back, this Razor. I'll hit your line once I have all my ducks in a row."**

"Aight, son. Just remember, if push comes to shove and the family route don't work, you know how we get down. At the end of the day, the only real family you got is me, everyone else is replaceable. Ya dig me?"

"Heard." I clicked over to end the call and Razor spoke.

"Damn, nigga, what took you so long?"

"Was on the phone with Pops. Wassup? And make it quick, I'm at my mom's crib."

"Aight, so I went over to the hospital and spoke to my boy's girl." He stopped talking as if he was letting me digest what he had to say.

"Okay, and what?" I urged him to continue.

"Maan, we dealing with some thorough bitches, forreal. According to Journey, they popped my boy right in front of her and then knocked her in the head with something before leaving. She say it was three bitches, but she couldn't make out the faces."

"Hmm, she tell them anything?"

"She can't tell them something she don't know nothing about. She did say that before they popped him, he mentioned his cousin having his car. She been tryna call dude but no answer."

"Aight, well keep looking into it and keep me updated."

"Got you. Ay, how shit going on your end? Seem like we may have stepped into some shit with your sister. It's even more clear

that they don't fuck around, at all. I lowkey like how they moving. Might just have to pull up on one of them myself if you know what I mean."

I ran my hand across my braids, pondering the thought. "That might not be a bad idea but hold that thought for now. At the present moment, I have to plant some seeds, water them, and see how they grow. It won't be as smooth of a transition as I thought it would be, I know that."

"I hear you. Let me ask you this though, if it comes down to it and she don't willingly give you that spot—."

"Then, I'ma *take* it," I cut him off.

"Good. I was just checking the temperature. I'll hit you once I have more info and track this nigga down."

"Aight. Just continue to keep a low profile. I'ma make something shake for us real soon."

"Yeah, do that. I ain't come on the East Coast to sit on my hands, my boy. You know I still got a standby and a wish to throw in the wishing well if need be."

"Yeah, I know. And we're gonna use it when the time calls for it. Right now, we just gotta play this shit by ear, trust me. In the meantime, tell your people to keep their ears to the streets and their eyes on the prize, feel me?"

"I'm already knowin'. They on the job as we speak."

"Then we good. I'll get up witchu soon." I ended the call and pushed my phone down in my pocket. Putting both conversations with my pops and Razor to the back of my mind, I headed back inside to play the role of the son who longed for his family.

"Oh, hey baby. I was just coming to look for you," Renee said as I reentered the house.

Closing the door behind me, I pulled her by her waist and kissed her neck. She giggled lightly and pulled back from my embrace.

"Y'all started eating?"

"Of course not. We were waiting on you. Everything good?"

"It will be," I gave a short answer.

"So, everything's not okay?" She questioned again with inquisitive eyes.

"Everything is what it's supposed to be at this time. We'll talk more about it later."

I kissed her cheek and grabbed her hand, escorting her back to where she'd walked off with Asia earlier.

"Oh, good," Asia let out from her seat next to my mother. "I was about to suggest that we eat without you, dad."

"Damn, you was gon' do me like that?" I pulled out a chair for Renee and sat next to her, admiring the spread in front of me.

"Dad, look at this food. I would've had to take a bite of one of those Hawaiian rolls or sumn'." We all laughed at her sincere face.

"And Gran was sure gon' let you, boo," my mother backed her. "You got us waiting here, stomach touching our backs and shit. Let's say grace and we can dig in." She held her hand out for me to take and I did. We all bowed and I waited for the prayer.

"God Did!" Asia yelled out and I cracked up laughing.

"Oh, yeah, she is definitely you at that age," my mother commented while smiling. "And that's just how Mahogany is with her daughter."

"I wish she could've stayed," Renee spoke. "Santana was really looking forward to this." I wanted to tell her to ease back on making it seem as if I was begging to be accepted, but I let her make it.

My mother nodded and placed her napkin in her lap. "Well, I ain't gon' lie to you, boo. There's a chance that she may not wanna have anything to do with Santana at all." I could tell by Renee's face that she was shocked at her bluntness, but I wasn't, so I let her continue. "Look, Mahogany has a warm heart but the way this reunion came about was sudden for her. The best thing to do now is give her time."

"I respect that, ma," I said with fake sincerity. "I can't even blame her for how she feels, I would've had the same energy. All I want is my family together. It's been far too long and I want my daughter to know her people."

"Yeah, and I don't have much family, so I want our daughter to know all of the people that make up her village," Renee added. She was laying it on too thick in my opinion and I knew my mother's bullshit meter was probably going off.

"Maaan, we gon' figure it out. Right now, let's eat before my baby pass out over there." I pointed over at Asia and she nodded in agreement.

I'd eat at my mother's dinner table tonight and plan to take over The Table tomorrow. I thought to myself as I dug into my prime cut steak.

Chapter Two
CURTIS "COOLIE" WRIGHT

*"**What you think, Dough?**" I asked Dorian once* Santana disconnected the call.

He paused before speaking, likely gathering his thoughts, and digesting the conversation. That was Dough. He always processed before giving his opinion on any situation. Clearing his throat, he finally put words to his thoughts. **"I don't trust that lil' nigga. Then again, I don't trust nobody."**

*"**Damn, not even me?**" I faked hurt.*

*"**Nigga, especially you. You've been on bullshit since I met yo' ass.**" We both shared a genuine laugh.* **"How you hanging in there, man?"**

*"**Man, you know me. These bars ain't bout shit. Now, the people behind them is a whole different story. A whole bunch of young, ignorant motherfuckas behind these walls. They ain't got shit to live for and don't respect a damn thing."**

*"**I already know. That ain't no place for you to be, man. As levelheaded as you are, it don't take much for shit to go sideways with you."**

*"**As true as that statement is, you know I don't let niggas***

beneath me get under my skin. I hope y'all ain't out there worrying about me."

"Shit, I ain't. I can't say the same for Mahogany. You know Antoinette out here holding it down."

Dough was my boy and had been for the last twenty plus years. I never had to question his character or his judgement when it came to business or personal matters. I knew that when my sentence was handed down to me that my family was in good hands. And if the shoe was on the other foot, he'd be able to say the same. Not only was Dough loyal but he respected my position and played his.

"Yeah. My babygirl ready to shut down anything moving behind her OG. Back to Santana, though."

"Don't trust 'em. You gotta think, he's been around his puss-ass, jealous ass daddy for the last decade or so. And you know what they say—."

"Birds of a feather flock together?"

"Nah. They say if you raised by a flawed ass individual, the likelihood of you becoming one is in the 99th percentile."

"That's what they say, huh?"

"Shiidd, I ain't never known them to be wrong when it comes to these matters." Again, I laughed.

"Nigga, who are the them and they?"

"They is I, and I is them." We both cracked up at his witty sense of humor.

"Well, putting him on with Mahogany should reveal his true intentions. I'm giving him the benefit of doubt seeing as so many years have passed. We haven't met Santana the man, we only know Santana the boy."

"Even more of a reason why you need to rethink putting him on," Dough expressed.

"That's why Mahogany is in position. It's her job to rule out deceit."

"And if you detect any larceny in Santana's heart?"

I answered his question without hesitation. *"I'll be the shoulder for Nette to cry on at his funeral."* My declaration may have been harsh, but no one would put my family in harm's way and live to tell the story.

"You know I don't doubt your decisions so long as it makes sense to me. Are you gonna put Mahogany up on game?"

"About who Santana is or me sending him her way?"

"Shit, both. You know she hates to be blindsided. She'll fuck around and kill that nigga and not bat an eyelash." He chuckled and I smiled at my daughter being just as savage as me.

"Yeah, I'll talk to her. I don't think it's best for me to reveal who he is just yet, though. That way if it turns out that he's back with ulterior motives, she can treat him accordingly."

"Aight, about that other business."

Knowing what he was referring to, I stopped the conversation before it could begin.

"Everything will work itself out, Dough."

"I know. You always say that shit, knowing that I have the ability to expedite things in an orderly fashion."

"You ain't never known me to lie, bruh. You know I'ma NWP. Nigga Wit' A Plan."

"Indeed. You know Hogany caught a body in the city recently. Popped the lil' nigga Yasir in broad daylight."

Yasir was one of the fugazy ass witnesses on my case. I'd specifically told Mahogany to leave the case alone, but she was both my child and her mother's, determined and hardheaded.

"Clean up?" I inquired.

"Yeah. You know we still have eyes on the ground and I'm sure Dudas did his part."

"Cool. I'll talk to her. I know time has passed but I still don't want bodies dropping back-to-back all of a sudden. This shit is already sensitive as it is."

"Aight, well I'll give it another week or so for the next one."

"Nigga."

He snickered. *"Aight, man. I'll stand down. Love, my boy."*

"Love."

While getting ready for my visit with my forever love, I thought about the last conversation I had with Dough. I heard his concerns, and he made a valid point when it came to Santana's bitch ass daddy. During Santana's childhood, years after he was released from prison, that nigga tried his best to cause friction in my household. It started with him trying to frustrate Nette by questioning her about how I dealt with Santana. Then trying to assert his role all the way in another state. I shut that shit down immediately. Wasn't no man about to dictate how I ran shit in my house, with my family, his kid included.

I ain't know what that nigga had going on, but my resume spoke for itself. I was known to get a nigga touched for merely even thinking I was something to play with. I wasn't problematic and that's exactly what he wanted, problems. I made sure not to let it affect my relationship with Santana, though. I still let him ride around with me and gave him little nuggets about the game.

We had a bond before his dad made an appearance and I didn't let the adult shit taint that. So, when he decided he wanted to move out to Cali to live with his donor, I supported it 100%. I had yet to find out the kind of person he'd groomed him to be. I only knew that me and his mom had given him a solid kid then.

I'd taken a couple days to go over the pros and cons of having Santana around now. I reasoned that not only would it give Nette and Mahogany the opportunity to get to know him again, but he could possibly be put on as another means of protection. With me giving him a fair shot in mind, I called off the extra pair of eyes I had on him since he landed back in town.

I wanted him to have a warm welcome and I knew that Antoinette was going to want the same after he reached out to her. What I didn't expect was for him to reach out to Mahogany so soon and witness a shootout that she was involved in. I was close to breaking the fuck out when I got the call from Santana detailing what had gone down. While he assured me that Mahogany had handled herself along with her crew and added that he'd let off a few shots of his own, it did nothing to ease my rage.

This was my motherfuckin' daughter we were talkin' about. Someone was going to answer for the threat to her life. Before I could get the ball rolling on tracking down the shooter, Santana provided the license plate number for the car that fled the scene. I put my resources to work and had the information in under two hours which I disclosed to Mahogany.

See, while I had no concerns about my daughter's ability to protect herself, she was still my baby. At any point I felt the need to step in, you better know I was gonna do that without a second thought. I was ten toes down about mine. I could tell that she didn't like the fact that I'd gotten the information before her but what really caught her by surprise was the messenger.

It was never my intention to reveal who Santana was, not this soon anyway. Like I told Dough, I wanted Mahogany to feel Santana out first. That way she could do business with a sound mind and not think with her heart. The night that everything had gone down, I called Antoinette to put her up on game. I told her it was time to rip the band aid off and to expect some questions from our daughter that only she could answer.

She knew the day would come where she'd have to explain to Mahogany who Santana was and that whole backstory. Neither of us could've predicted that a shooting at Mahogany's club would be the catalyst for the long overdue talk.

"Wright, visitor!" I turned around to acknowledge the C.O's presence and waited for the cell doors to pop before I approached.

The rules were different here at Green Haven State Prison. Being on the West Coast was too far for my liking and seeing as I didn't have a record, there was no need to have me in a max prison outside of the murder charges. I had my lawyer put in a transfer request citing that I needed to be closer to my family. I knew it was a long shot, but money talked, and my lawyer had the gift of gab. In two weeks' time, I was back on the East Coast.

I'd been locked up in California on two bodies over a year ago and hauled off to San Quentin State Prison. I just so happened to be in Cali working on a legal business deal when they bust into the restaurant, guns drawn, and a warrant for my arrest. When the detectives read off the charges, I got a good laugh. I sat high enough to where a nigga couldn't even pay me to get my hands dirty.

The only time I put in work was when I deemed it necessary. So, me being caught up on a murder charge let alone two was comical. I didn't argue nor try to plead my case. I waited for the pigs in a blanket to give me my phone call and dialed Dough's number. I gave instructions and not even 24 hours later, my lawyers were on a plane, and I was bonded out. During my time out on bond, my lawyers along with a few other sources did what they were paid to do, find information.

I had the names of the deceased and the witnesses who'd placed me at the scene of the crime which according to the detectives was committed in New York. My lawyers made it clear that with those testimonies from five different individuals, there was no way that I'd get off scott free. And to hear that from the best, I took their word and told them to do everything they could and then some. I sat Antoinette and Mahogany down first and gave it to them straight just as my lawyers had done me. Mahogany's first reaction was to get rid of the witnesses and all would be good. I quickly shut her idea down. I didn't want my name tied to any more bullshit, although I knew it would've been handled quickly and she would've made a bold statement.

I'd been operating in the game for over two decades and had remained untouched. I reasoned that it was time for me to sit. After assuring them that I wouldn't be gone for long, I laid out instructions for how we would move going forward. They listened intently and agreed not to question my decision.

Dough thought I was crazy as hell, and like Mahogany, he had the idea to do away with the witnesses. I let him know that someone had orchestrated this whole thing, and they'd reveal themselves soon enough. Until then, it was a waiting game. A long, uncomfortable one, but a waiting game, nonetheless. You could never keep a solid nigga down.

"After all these years, these bitches still ain't got nothin' on you, Queen." I praised my better half as she walked into my awaiting arms for a much-needed hug. Even dressed down in a pair of jeans and a t-shirt, none of the women in the visiting room could hold a candle to mine.

"Had it then, still having shit now, baby," she replied cockily. "You know that ain't gon' never change. I told you that when we said our vows. How you holding up, King?" I kissed her lips twice and smiled while nodding, remembering when we got married.

During our vows, Antoinette promised to always be the baddest bitch walking for as long as we both shall live. The whole church got a kick out of that and even the officiant had to laugh. My wife was a spitfire. Antoinette was my rock, my best kept secret, and above all, she was my person.

"I keep telling you to stop worrying about me woman. I'm good so long as y'all are great." I held my hand out for her to take hold of as we sat down. "So, are y'all great?"

"We're great, baby. We had dinner with Santana last night. Well, let me correct myself, *I* had dinner with Santana and his family. Our daughter canceled on me at the last minute."

"She didn't show up?"

"No, she showed up. She just picked up Beautii and left."

I squeezed her hand and put it up to my lips to kiss it. "I didn't expect anything different, baby."

She sucked her teeth. "Yeah, that's your child, stubborn as hell. Had she stayed she would've seen that she and Santana have that similarity as well."

"When she's ready, baby. You may have to give her a minute though, especially after what just transpired."

"Yeah, speaking of that. Santana mentioned what had gone down and wanted to know how I felt about him sticking around to look after Hogany. After having witnessed her in action, he just feels that it wouldn't hurt to have him as a part of the collective, ya know. The more family, the better, right."

"Oh yeah?" I sat back in the chair and rubbed my goatee. Santana hadn't mentioned that he posed the idea of being a part of The Table to his mother. I took it as him trying to get her vote of confidence.

She nodded. "I don't think it's a bad idea, baby. This way we don't have to worry so much about her."

"You mean, *you* don't have to worry. I know Mahogany can take care of herself and she has a team of killers at her disposal. Coupled with Tiffany and Morae, she's good."

"I hear you, babe, but if he's willing to uproot his family to come back here and be a part of our family, both business and personal, I won't talk him out of it."

"Never asked you to, love."

"I know, but—."

"Don't go back and forth with me, Queen. You know how I feel about that." I signaled with my hand that the conversation was over.

"How they been treating you in here?" She changed the subject, and it was a good thing she did.

One thing I wasn't gonna do was go back and forth with my wife. Whether behind bars or out on the street, I demanded a certain respect at all times. The rest of the visit went well with her catching me up on her comings and goings as well as our legitimate businesses that she kept up in my absence. At the end of our visit, we circled back around to Mahogany, Santana, and The Table. I made it clear that Mahogany wasn't going to give Santana a free ride because of who he was.

If anything, she was going to see to it that he worked twice as hard, and I expected nothing less. Santana may have been a gangsta and a mover and shaker back in Cali, but he was back on the East Coast now. He'd have to play by the Wright rules.

Chapter Three

MAHOGANY

Leaving my mother's house, the interaction with Santana replayed in my head. Nothing in me felt the family attachment. No flashbacks of my childhood came to mind either. For the most part, I drew a blank. Santana, on the other hand, was full of discoveries and attempts to walk me down memory lane. He wanted to share experiences that I didn't remember and didn't care to pretend to.

He was trying to resume this big brother role that had been assigned to him by birth but not approved by me. The same sentiments I shared with my mother, I ran down to him. We didn't know each other and there was no need to pretend that I was open to forming the bond he was seeking. To be quite honest, I didn't know about him being a part of The Table either. He seemed too eager and, in my mind, an eager motherfucka was a *desperate* motherfucka.

While his outward appearance showed poise, it didn't match the words that left his mouth. He'd made his intentions clear; he wanted to get put on. I was quick to let him know that he didn't have to use "getting to know me" as a method to do so. He'd go through the preliminary screening which included meeting with my right and left hands and then I'd make the decision of whether or not we could do business.

Deciding that my night had enough excitement and turns of events, I kept our interaction short.

"Ma, Aunty Tiff is calling," Beautii pointed out to me while holding up my vibrating phone.

"Thanks, boo." Taking the phone from her, I hit the green phone button to answer.

"Wassup, Tiff?"

"Hey, you need to come back to Mo's crib. She just got into it with Paris and almost hit this girl in front of her son."

"Stop making up shit, Tiffany. You know if I wanted to hit that girl there would be nothing y'all could do to stop me." Morae spoke in a deadly but calm tone.

"Am I on speaker?" I asked, rerouting my car to head to Mo's house.

"Yeah," Tiffany confirmed.

"Mo, do I need to come over there?" I asked as if I hadn't already made the decision.

"You can come get your employee." Hearing her reference Paris as my employee with no emotion, let me know she was on one.

"You know that girl ain't have nothing to do with what her bd got going on. Don't do her like that." I argued on Paris' behalf.

"I know that, Hogany. I never said she had anything to do with it, but I know me. My brother just walked in here fresh out the precinct, my baby boy. I ain't gon' be laid up with her knowing what I got in store for her child's father. And you know I ain't hiding shit. Soon as she tries to talk me down, ain't no telling what I might do. It's best she go about her business while I tend to mine."

"You know that girl love you, Mo."

"Yeah, but I love my brother more. That shit said, ain't no relationship until I get this figured out. Ain't no way up, down, or around that, Mahogany."

I sighed because it was a tough situation to be in, but I understood. The bond that Mo shared with her brothers was something I'd never seen before. You could tell they all were brought up close knit and came from the same mama and daddy. **"I respect that. I'll be there shortly. Tiff, take me off speaker please."**

"Yeah."

"Did she really try to hit her?"

"No. I dragged that part. They had a stare off, though. Paris wasn't backing down either."

I smiled a little, liking that Paris was willing to go toe to toe over her love.

"Stop talkin' shit like I ain't right here, hoe." I heard Mo say.

"Girl, I ain't scared, da fuck," Tiff fired back.

"Y'all chill out. I'll be there in a minute."

"And when you get here, take her and Money with you. They think I'm stupid, I know they fucked in here. Money walkin' round here with his eyes glued to her. His goofy ass almost tripped over his own damn feet."

"What?! We did not!" Tiffany's voice went up two octaves, giving away her guilt.

I sighed at her practically telling on her damn self.

"I knew it!" Mo yelled out and I ended the call, refusing to referee an argument between the two of them over the phone.

"We going to Aunty Mo's house?" Beautii asked, securing my phone in the cup holder.

"You a nosey somethin'," I said and she giggled.

"What? Y'all the ones who talk all loud."

"Yeah, well close yo' ears when I'm on the phone, Nosetta." Taking one hand off the steering wheel, I tickled her.

"Okay, okay," she chuckled, squirming in her seat. "I'll stop being nosey."

"You sure?"

"Yesss, ma, pleaseee." Satisfied with her response, I stopped tickling her.

"Cool, we good then." Stopping at a red light, I reached out to play with Beautii's ponytail.

While doing so, I looked out her window just as a blacked-out Dodge Charger pulled up alongside of us. I took note of the car's heavy tint and for some reason, I felt sudden flutters in my stomach. It put me on high alert.

"Ma, we're having a daddy/daughter dance at my school next month and I want daddy to come. You think he'll have time?"

I half listened to Beautii as I pressed the gas on my car once the light turned green. The Dodge waited for the car behind me to move before changing lanes, falling in line behind it. I gripped the steering wheel tight but kept my facial expression light and posture straight as to not alert Beautii.

"Ma," she called out to me, "you think daddy will be able to make it to the dance?"

"Not sure, baby. We can reach out to him, though. As a matter of fact, give him a call now." Briscoe wanted me to keep him in the loop, this was me doing just that.

In my rearview mirror I could see the Charger switching lanes quickly before jumping in front of the second driver so that it was now tailing me. Nodding, I reached under my seat and pulled out my F&N.

"He didn't answer, ma. You want me to send him a text?"

"No. Beautii."

"Huh?" She looked over at me and her eyes zeroed in on the gun on my lap before meeting my face again.

"Remember those emergency situations me, you, and Gran talk about every now and then?" She nodded, showing her understanding with no fear in her eyes. "This is one of those situations. I need you to take your seatbelt off and get down on the floor, understand?"

"Yes, mommy. You want me to call Aunty Tiff?" She asked while unsnapping her seatbelt.

"Yeah, boo, and put the call on speaker for me." At nine years old, my baby was already thinking on her feet.

And while I never glorified my dealings in the street or even had Beautii bear witness to it, some things were unavoidable. I put a little speed on the Tesla and at this point, the Dodge was no longer trying to hide the fact that it was openly following me as the car accelerated with me.

"Hey, Beautii girl, everything okay?"

"Tiff, we got a situation and I'm bout to do damage. I need you to meet me on—."

"Ahhh!" Beautii yelled out as we were hit from behind, making the car swerve a little.

"I know the fuck this bitch ass...hold on, Beautii."

"Drop yo location. I'm on my way. Beautii, be strong." Just as quick as she answered, Tiff hung up.

Keeping my hand steady on the wheel, I could see the car pull up on the side of me. I anticipated his next move was to try and run me off the road and I couldn't have that. I didn't give a fuck about any other drivers at that point, it was about me and my baby getting out of this jam. Putting it on the line, I lowered my window and without a thought, I aimed and sent two shots into the passenger side window of the car and one shot to the tire. The car swerved and hit another, giving me a clearing for escape.

I did just that and took the closest exit, getting the fuck out of dodge. Making my way onto a residential street, I glanced down to check on Beautii and she was staring right up at me with tears in her eyes. Reaching down, I grabbed her hand and squeezed it tightly. I wanted so bad to cry but the tears wouldn't come. Whoever was out there deciding that they wanted my attention, they sure as hell had it now, even more than before.

"Y'all okay?" Tiff asked, hopping out of Mo's car with Mo right behind her.

"Yeah, we good." I spoke for the both of us. I had Beautii sitting in my lap. It was the only way I could think of comforting her at the moment. Mo opened my door, letting Beautii out, and I grabbed my purse and any other personal effects. "I gotta do something about this car. Here, take this." I handed Tiff the F&N. She took it and tucked it behind her back.

"It's already taken care of. You wanna scrap it or have it put up?" Mo asked.

"Who you got to pick it up?"

"Ron," she answered. Ron was one of her people, so I knew I was in good hands.

"Have him tow it to my mechanic and drop it in his yard. I'll make the call and handle the rest. Thanks, Mo."

"You know you don't even have to do all that. Come on, Beautii." She escorted Beautii to the backseat of her car.

I threw my head back and sighed with my eyes closed. When I opened them, Tiffany stared at me.

"Come on, let's get away from this hot ass car," she stated and walked around to the driver's side.

Saying nothing else, I hopped into the backseat with Beautii and she laid her head on my shoulder. I kissed her forehead and held her hand. "It'll never happen again," I whispered to her. She didn't respond verbally, but I felt her scoot closer to me and took that as a sign that she took in what I said.

My vibrating phone interrupted the still silence that filled the car, making Beautii jump a little. Her reaction was unsettling. Wrapping my arm around her, I pulled my phone from my bag and identified the incoming call from Justice. Not up for idle chit chat, I declined the call and went to put the phone away, only for him to call again.

"Justice, right now is not the time. I have something going on that requires my full attention at the moment," I let out before he could get a word in.

"Respect. I was just reaching out to see if you made it home safely." I don't know why, but after what had happened on the highway, I wasn't feeling him questioning my whereabouts.

"Nah, I haven't made it there just yet. I had a bump in the road but nothing I couldn't handle." I made it clear in case he was on some fuck shit.

"Oh, yeah? Anything I can help with?"

I paused before saying what was on my mind then thought, *fuck it.* **"Yeah, as a matter of fact, you can. Do you know anyone who owns a black, tinted out Dodge Charger?"**

He chuckled lightly. **"That's quite specific don't you think? But, to answer your question, I'm sure there's two hundred plus**

people in New York City alone that own the vehicle you just described.”

“Hmm, minus one,” I replied.

“Come again?” He questioned; confusion settled in his tone.

“Hogany—.” I held up my hand to stop Mo from speaking and pointed to my phone.

“Justice, let me hit you back.”

“Aight, beautiful.” He disconnected the call, and I dropped my phone in my lap.

“Turn on your police scanner real quick, Mo.” Pulling the scanner out, she did as I asked and as expected, I could hear the police dispatcher calling for assistance on the Westside highway. “Call Du—.”

“Already on it,” Mo said. “I sent him a text and I’m waiting on his reply.”

“You need to call him,” Tiffany spoke up. “This shit needs to be addressed asap and a text message ain’t gon’ cut it. Motherfuckas out here losing they rabbit ass mind. We ain’t never been tried on this level.”

“Ears, Tiff.” I gave her a quick glance and then looked down at Beautii to remind her that my frazzled daughter was still present. She stopped talking and proceeded to pull up in front of Mo’s place. “Have Monk Man or Money come down and get Beautii, Mo. I need to talk to you and Tiff.”

“I’ll take her up and come back down. Paris was packing her things when we left. Maybe seeing me come in and leave again will make her move faster.”

“Damn, I forgot she was still there. Let me call her to come down.” I went to pick up my phone and thought better of it. “Matter fact, come on, let’s all get out.” We went to step out of the car and my phone rang. I didn’t recognize the number, but I wasn’t into ducking calls, so I answered.

“Who dis?”

“The grim reaper, bitch. Duck.” The line went dead and I didn’t think twice before snatching Beautii back as she walked towards Mo’s open arm and hit the pavement.

“Ground!” I yelled just as shots rang out.

I couldn't make out where they were coming from and didn't lift my head to check as I shielded Beautii's body with mine. Hearing the bullets tear into the car and Beautii's loud screams, I felt as if I was having an outer body experience. When the shots finally stopped, it felt like my heart was beating on Beautii's shoulder, that's how close I held her to me.

"Tiff!" I heard Mo yell out. I didn't want to look in the direction of where she was screaming, but my eyes had a mind of their own as they opened and followed her feet as she rushed over to Tiffany who was laid out on the ground with the F&N clutched in her hand.

"Ain't no fuckin' way," I thought to myself as tears pooled in my eyes and I went tone death, drowning out Mo's cries for help.

Chapter Four

MONEY

I sat on the couch in Mo's living room with DJ in my lap, watching Paris gather her things and slowly place them into her bag with her head hung low. Lowkey, I felt bad for her. I knew my sister could be difficult and often cold-hearted once she felt wronged in any way. And although we all knew that Paris didn't have anything to do with Monk Man getting locked up, what happened was a direct result of being with her. Of course, P didn't understand that, but I knew there was no changing Mo's mind about it at the moment.

And to be honest, as bad as I felt for Paris, there wasn't an ounce of forgiveness for her bd. I had plans to fuck that nigga ova something serious. There was no way around that. He crossed a line and had made himself a threat and we exterminated niggas like that.

"Here, let me help you," I offered and sat DJ down on the couch next to me.

"No, Money. I got it!" She snapped and snatched her bag up from the floor. "Damn," she sighed, dropping the bag. "I'm sorry. I didn't mean to snap on you like that."

"You good, sis." I gave her a half hug and she wiped her eyes before I could see a tear drop.

"I didn't mean for any of this to happen, Money. I love your sister with everything in me. You think she'll come around to at least hearing that from me?" Her sincere eyes searched mine for an answer that would lessen the blow of their break/breakup.

"I can't call it, P," I answered honestly. "This some real shit that went down. I mean, our little brother was taken out of here in cuffs. Some shit is just unforgivable."

She nodded solemnly. "I understand. I'm gonna do my best to fix this. Monk Man is like a brother to me. I don't know what type of shit Derek on, but he took it too far and I'm gonna check him about it."

"You just focus on my lil' man, DJ, here. Don't worry bout nothin' else. It'll be taken care of."

"Do I even wanna know what that means?"

"Shit, do you? Cause you know I ain't gon' sugar coat nothin' for you, P. You also know how we are when it comes to our own. Nobody gets a pass and that blood gon' always be thicker than water, feel me."

She glanced over at DJ who sat on the couch swinging his feet and then back at me. My stare was unwavering. I know what I said, and she knew exactly what I meant. Without another word, she went to pick her bag up and shots rang out. On instinct, I pulled DJ from the couch and onto the floor.

"Get down!" I yelled out to her as she stood frozen before hitting the ground. I called out for Monk Man to stay wherever he was in the house.

"DJ!" Paris cried out from the side of the couch where she took cover. She went to pop her head up and the base in my tone stopped her.

"Stay down, P!" It was clear that the shots were coming from outside, but the shits sounded so close, I wanted to make sure we all stayed planted until the shots halted.

After about a minute or so, the gunfire ceased. I counted 30 seconds in my head before raising up with DJ in my arms. At the same time Monk Man appeared from the back of the house with his gun by his side. Mo and I made it a point to teach him how to shoot when he turned ten, so he knew his way around an array of guns. We were in the street and made sure he was prepared for whatever.

"What the hell, bro?!" He let out while making his way over to the window.

"Fuck is you doin', bro. Getcho ass from in front of the window!" I barked on Monk Man and pulled my ringing phone from my pocket. **"Mo, where y'all a—."**

"Come downstairs now! Tiffany was hit!" Her words hit my chest and my heart rate quickened.

"I'm coming. Don't hang up the phone!" Turning to Monk Man, I pointed to Paris. "Hold her down and don't answer your phone for nobody but me or Mo, do you understand me?" He nodded. I went to head for the door and Paris called out to me.

"Wait, Money, what's wrong? Where's Morae?"

Ignoring her, I walked out of the house and took the steps downstairs. I needed to get to my baby.

"I got you, Tiff. We gon' getchu to a hospital, boo." Hearing Mo talk to Tiff as if she was about to take her last breath pissed me off.

"Aye, stop fuckin' talkin' to her like she bout to die or somethin', man. She gon' be good!" There was no doubt in my mind about that. My baby was a gangsta.

Making it down to the lobby, I took note of the crowd in front of the building.

"Move the fuck back!" I could hear Mahogany bark at the murmuring crowd who hadn't attempted to offer their assistance.

Hanging up on Mo, I pushed through the crowd, and nothing could prepare me for what I saw. Even though night had fallen, it seemed as though there was an illuminating light on Tiffany. The love of my life lay sprawled out on the ground while Mo kneeled over her with her hands pressed against her chest. I could see the blood pouring through her fingers and in that moment, I knew I had to snap out of my trance and snap into action. Every second that she lay on the ground with blood seeping out of her chest was a second too long for me.

"Back up, Mo," I said, rushing over to pick Tiffany up.

"I called for an ambulance," Mahogany advised me.

"I *am* the fuckin' ambulance," I countered. "Where's the car?" The hospital wasn't too far from Mo's crib and with the way I planned on driving, I was going to cut the time in half anyway.

"Over here," Mahogany instructed. We ran over to the car, and she tossed me the keys. "Mo, take Beautii upstairs and I'm gonna ride with them."

I was so focused on Tiff that I didn't even notice Beautii. Gently placing Tiff in the backseat, Mahogany got in with her and before she could close the door, I was already pulling off. I had a one-track mind and that was making sure that my baby lived to be by my side to go to war with the motherfucka who tried to take her out.

"My girl was shot. I need help now!" My voice boomed as I rushed into the emergency room of the hospital with Tiff in my arms.

"Sir, wait, let me get a stretcher for you," one of the hospital personnel said to me with her hands up. I wasn't tryna hear that shit. At this point, I was tryna walk Tiff to the back myself.

"I don't have time for all that. My girl is bleeding out."

"Here, Synclair." A woman dressed in blue scrubs said to the older lady standing in front of me who wore the same uniform in a different color. She pushed a stretcher in my direction and instructed me to lay Tiffany down on it.

"Okay, sir, we got it from here. Let us take care of her." I kissed Tiffany's forehead and grabbed the woman by her wrist. Not hard enough to hurt her, but enough to get her attention.

"On my unborn child, if that woman don't survive..."

"We're gonna do everything we can. You have my word." I nodded at her declaration, hoping she knew that she was gonna have to stand on that. I wasn't the type of nigga that you could just say anything to. Your word was your bond.

I let her go and she followed behind the lady who'd come with the stretcher, and they disappeared into the back. I felt a hand on my shoulder and turned to find Mahogany next to me.

"Let me talk to you outside for a minute."

"Respectfully, Hogany, I'm not leaving this area until I find out what's going on with her."

"It wasn't a request Money. I need to talk to you outside." She went to walk off ahead of me and I followed. We stepped outside of the hospital doors and into a dimly lit corner. "Look, I don't know what the fuck is going on and who's coming at me, but I got a call just before the shots rang out. Someone also tried to run me off the road tonight. I took care of that situation, though. This shit that happened with Tiffany getting hit up is my fault and I'm gonna take care of it."

"Oh yeah?" I questioned. "Since when they put an I in team? We in this shit together, which means we gon' deliver the death sentences together, feel me." When I pledged myself to The Table, I knew I was gonna be ten toes down with no questions asked. More than that, Mahogany was family, so if someone was coming for her, they were coming for us.

"You sound like Tiffany." She cracked a small smile, but the sadness was evident in her tone. "You know she gon' pull through, right."

"She got to. We having a baby."

"A baby?" She questioned, confused, and likely wanting to call bullshit.

"Yeah. Can't get into that right now, though. You checked in with Dudas to see if there's any word on what happened on the highway or shit, what happened at the club? It's too much going on. A nigga feel like he getting a migraine." I rubbed my head.

"I'ma bout to get on the horn and see now. Mo had texted him. We haven't heard anything back yet."

"Say that. Ay, you think Paris' bd had anything to do with this shit? You know, with the shooting happening right outside of Mo's building."

"You know everybody is guilty until proven innocent. And although I don't think his bitch ass got the heart to even try some shit like this, he's on my shit list."

"Cool, so I can dead that nigga then."

"Nah, you can't." I wanted to say something in protest, but she beat me to talking. "Mo's gonna take care of that how she sees fit." She glanced down at her phone and then back up to me. "You good here? I gotta take care of something. Let me get the car keys."

I handed them to her. "You know I ain't going nowhere. I'll keep you posted."

"Okay, cool." She hugged me around my neck and let out a sigh. "Don't call me with no bad news, Montez."

"Not if I can help it." Releasing me, she made her way back to the car and I waited until she pulled off before reentering the hospital.

Walking up to the front desk, I asked the receptionist if there were any updates on Tiff as of yet.

"She just went back, sir. I'm sure the doctors are doing everything they can. In the meantime, can we have her name and date of birth?" I gave her the information and she typed it into her computer. "I do want to let you know that it is hospital protocol to alert the authorities when we have a gunshot victim. I'll—."

"Do you have a napkin?" I asked, cutting her off.

"Oh, sure." She set a box of Kleenex on top of the counter and pushed it towards me. I took the box of tissues and went into my pocket. "Like I was saying, we have to alert the authorities. I can give you a minute before I do so. I did hear you mention that the victim was your girlfriend."

"She is and Maya, is it?" I asked, reading her name tag.

"Yes, that's me."

"I'd appreciate it if you held off on that call altogether." I pushed the tissue box back to her and inside was the couple hundred dollars I had in my pocket. I nodded towards it and her eyes widened. "That cool?"

"Umm, uhh, yeah, I can hold off. I can't say what the doctors or nurses will do, though."

"Don't worry bout that, shorty. Just do your part. I appreciate it." She was a young girl, probably in her early twenties. I knew the money would keep her quiet.

I tapped the counter and went to take a seat. I couldn't believe that I was actually in the waiting room of a hospital while my baby was on somebody's surgery table fighting. I thought back to the first time I saw Tiffany buss her gun and knew at that moment that I was in love with her.

"Montez, get in the car... we don't have all day," Tiff yelled out to me

from the window of her Range Rover as I exited my building. She was so damn impatient.

"Chill out with all that, woman. I don't live in the ghetto and I don't want the people that live in this building to think my lady ghetto either." I hopped into the passenger seat and leaned in to kiss her.

"I'm not in the mood, Montez, forreal. Close the door so we can go." As always, she dubbed my shit. I only laughed and closed the door like she said. "Put your seatbelt on, please."

"So, you care about my safety, but a nigga can't get a kiss? You ass backwards as hell."

"I'm tellin' you to put your seatbelt on because I'm bout to drive this fuckin' car like we on the "Jetsons" and I don't want you to fly out this window."

"Okay, nothin' in your statement countered what I just said. You care about a nigga." I reached over and grabbed her hand.

"Boy, get off my hand." She shook me off and her tires burned rubber, peeling out of the parking spot. "How many times I gotta remind you that I have a man?"

"Till' I give a fuck." I pulled out my phone and went to answer the slew of text messages from a few chicks I fucked with. I swore they had a nigga in a group chat somewhere cause they were saying the same shit. A whole bunch of nothing.

"Yes, please busy yourself with that phone cause I need to get my mind right."

"What's wrong?" I asked, putting my phone down.

She looked over at me. "Mahogany didn't tell you why she felt the need for you to ride with me?"

"No. She just called and told me she needed me to pull up with you somewhere."

"Yeah, well, one of our delivery drivers didn't deliver all of the product to its designated location and he's been ducking Mahogany's calls. We're going to pay him a visit to pay our respects."

"Oh, yeah? Who met their unfortunate demise due to his careless larceny?"

"The man that raised him."

"Damn. It's a cold world, ain't it?"

"That it is." She turned her music up and focused on the road. We pulled up to an address in Forest Hills an hour later. She parked in front of a single-family home and turned off the ignition. "Come on."

I followed behind her, admiring the way her hips swayed in her jeans. I just knew her nigga wasn't diggin' off in that ass the way he should've been because she was walkin' straight. Fuckin' with me, she'd have a permanent stank walk. I'd be tearing that ass out the frame every chance I got.

Making it to the front door, she rang the doorbell and stood back. No one answered for a moment, prompting her to ring the bell again.

"I'm coming!" A male's voice yelled out. Tiff glanced over at me and back at the door. "Here I come," the male said again. Opening the door, he quickly went to shut it once he noticed Tiff. My foot halted his attempt.

"Who the fuck just opens the door and not ask who it is? Especially when you know you've done some foul shit," Tiff chastised, pushing the door open. Dude was skinny as shit and looked like a smoker so when she pushed the door, he stumbled back a little.

"Tiffany, I—." He went to speak, and she cut him off.

"Don't wanna hear it, Reem. Just tell me where the product is, and I can go on about my day."

"It's in my truck. In the garage." In my head, I thought, "this nigga got to be the dumbest motherfucka on earth."

"Perfect. Let's go get it. You lead the way."

"Okay, come on. Follow me." He turned to walk and we were right behind him. "You know, it was really just an honest mistake. I was going to come see Mahogany at the club, then my dad got sick, so I've been taking care of him for the past week. You know I'm all he has after my mom passed." He talked fast as we moved through his kitchen to get to the side door that led us out to the garage.

"Reem, less talking and more getting what I came for," Tiff let out in a dead tone.

"Right," he responded. I stood off to the side and watched as he popped his trunk and there the brick stood, exposed with nothing covering it.

"Really nigga?" I let out. "You gon' make it easy for a nigga to steal from you after tryna steal from us? Oh, you a **real** dummy." I shook my head.

"He...he..here you go," he stuttered, handing the brick to Tiff who handed it to me. As he went to close the trunk, she spoke.

"Reem."

"Huh?" He answered, looking up to find her .45 pointed at him. "Wait, hol' on. I gave you the product, Tiffany. Please don't do this." He held his hands up in the air as if they would stop the bullets and slowly walked backwards.

*"You know how you mentioned being all your dad has? I want you to go be with him, so he'll never be lonely." **POP! POP!** She sent two shots to his chest and his body hit the ground. Casually walking over to the body, she picked up her shell casings and pocketed them. "Ready?" She asked me.*

I adjusted my hard on, not bothering to hide it. "Yeah, I'm ready, ma." Smirking, she shook her head and after trashing the living room and kitchen to make the shooting look like a robbery gone wrong, we made our way out.

Yeah, that day solidified that she was *the one.*

"Sir," the Synclair woman called out to me. I made my way over to her and tried to gauge her facial expression. It was void of emotion for a second before she broke out in a small smile. "You got yourself a fighter. She pulled through."

I clasped my hands together and bit my lip. "That's what the fuck I'm talkin' bout! Woo!" I didn't give a damn about the stares I got in the waiting room; my baby had pulled through.

"They're patching up her chest now and she'll be put in a room to recover. I'll come back out to get you in a few."

"Preciate you." She gave me a smile and a nod before walking off.

I sent a text to Mo and Mahogany that Tiff was good and put my phone away. I would be here to nurse my baby back to health, but it was up the moment she was 100%.

Chapter Five

MORAE

"IT'S GONNA BE OKAY, AUNTY MO." BEAUTII'S VOICE HAD brought me back from the dark place in my mind where I'd watched blood spill from Tiffany's chest.

We were finally able to enter my building after pig patrol questioned me outside for about thirty minutes. My answers to them were straightforward; my friend was shot, and I didn't see anything after she hit the ground. I was too busy trying to keep her from bleeding out. I could tell they were fishing for more and even tried their luck by asking if they could question Beautii. After telling them to fuck off, they got the picture. The male detective handed me his card, gave his dry ass well wishes, and let me know that they would need to speak with me again soon.

My hands were shaking, and I had to take several deep breaths to calm myself down. Just looking down at Tiff and hearing the slow, shallow breaths she took shook me. For the short time we'd been operating The Table, no one had ever gon' head up with us at this level. Of course, we had our fair share of men who tested our gangsta and we were quick to check niggas. We gave little to no room for a nigga to even think he could play in our faces. What was going on currently was foreign.

And although I knew no one was untouchable, for us to be hit back-to-back, something had to give, and people had to die. It was an eye for an eye around these parts.

"I know, Babygirl, I know. Aunty Tiff is strong." I went to pull her in for a hug and she peered down at my hands. Remembering that they were still covered in Tiffany's blood, I pulled them back. "Shit, I'm sorry about that. You're strong, too, Beautii girl. I'm sorry you had to witness that." The elevator became quiet again as we rode up to my floor.

"Aunty," Beautii called out, "I don't want my mom to die. I don't want you or Aunty Tiff to die either." Hearing her speak those words followed by the tears that spilled from her eyes fucked me up.

Turning so that I was fully facing her, I leaned over so that we were face to face. "Real bitches don't die, boo. And me, mommy, and Tiff are as real as they come so I don't see us going anytime soon, you hear me."

She nodded. "I hear you."

"Alright, now wipe that pretty little face of yours." After making sure that her face was void of any tears, I asked if she was okay.

"Not really. I'm gonna call my mom and check on her when we get inside."

"That's a good idea." Getting off the elevator, I went to stick my key in the door, and it swung open.

"Oh my God. I thought something happened to you!" Paris exclaimed, throwing her arms around my neck.

"I'm good." I didn't let her settle into the hug before pulling myself from her embrace. "Beautii, go to the guest room and call your mom."

"Okay. Hey Paris, hey DJ." She gave Paris a wave and cooed at DJ who stood next to Paris, holding onto her pants leg.

"Hey, love. What the hell, Morae?! Whose blood is that on your hands?" Paris' shouting scared DJ, making him wail.

Cutting my eyes at her, I headed for the kitchen to wash my hands, being that it was the closest room with a sink in it.

"Sis, what's going on?" I heard Monk Man ask from behind me as I scrubbed my hands clean.

"I can't talk to you about that right now," I responded without turning around. I could feel him walk up on me and post up against the refrigerator, next to the sink.

"Mo, niggas were shooting outside and now you're washing blood off your hands." He gestured to the blood that flowed down the drain. "We don't have no choice but to talk about it now."

"Oh, so now you the parent?" I countered with a small chuckle to lighten the mood. Moreso for myself rather than him. I had to in order to keep from reverting back to the image of one of my best friends stretched out on the concrete with a gunshot to the chest.

"Forget it, I'll ask Money." He went to walk away, and I stopped him.

"Tiffany was shot. Money and Hogany took her to the hospital, and I have no word on her condition as of yet."

"Shot?!" Paris stood in the doorway of the kitchen with her hands covering her mouth.

Any other time, I wouldn't have mind discussing something so personal in her presence, but at the present time, we weren't in that space. And I didn't have room to give any thought as to how long I'd feel that way. We locked eyes and while mine held a dead stare, hers were pleading for a reaction from me. Specifically, something that said that we were okay. Only, we were anything but that.

"Damn, it's dad calling again." Monk Man held his phone up for me to see the incoming call from my father. Taking it from him, I answered it on speaker.

"Lil' nigga, I know you think you grown but when I call yo' phone, you stop whatever it is that you doing and answer the shit!" He was pissed and it made me wonder how many calls Monk Man had actually declined.

"Dad, it's me," I said, hoping my voice would make him ease up a bit. I went to leave the kitchen and gestured for Monk Man to follow, leaving Paris standing there, looking lost.

"I've been calling you, too. Shit, I called Money and Dudas. What I'm not understanding is why I can't reach none of y'all. Some shit is off, so someone better get to telling me what that is. And before you go to speak, just remember I can spot bullshit from a mile away." That was his subtle way of telling me not to lie.

"I got arrested," Monk Man blurted out and my head slowly turned towards him. The incredulous look on my face let him know that he'd fucked up. I used my hand to cover the speaker and punched him in his chest hard. "Ouch, what the fuck, Mo!"

"That's for being a dumbass," I whispered harshly. "Didn't nobody ask you to say shit, Monroe. Goddamn." I took the phone off speaker and put it to my ear.

"Morae Angel Thompson, you need to come see me. This is not a request. As a matter of fact, I'm calling a family meeting. And I mean *every* kid that I shot out of my ball sack better be there." I knew he meant business, but I was in no position to adhere to his demand at this time.

"Dad, right now, there's some heavy shit going on that I can't pull myself away from. I promise I'll come and see you once I get all my ducks in a row."

"See, where you fucked up was thinking this family shit was a democracy. I know the position you play at The Table but let's not forget the position *I* play at the head of this family, Morae." His voice was stern, and I knew there was no debating him.

"Da—."

"Nah," he cut me off. **"The conversation is done. Round your brothers up and I'll come to you."** He ended the call, and I closed my eyes and put my head back against the wall.

"What he say?" Monk Man inquired.

I sighed hard and opened my eyes. "He's coming over. And it's probably because your dumbass decided to spill the beans. You know to answer his calls every time, Monroe."

"Oh, yeah, I should've picked up when the shots were going off outside, right? That don't make no sense Mo." His argument made sense but shit, this was another issue I'd have to deal with. And I didn't want no smoke with my dad.

"Man, just check on Beautii for me. I'm gonna go have a conversation with Paris."

"Yeah, fix that."

"Nigga, stay in a child's place."

My phone chimed and I pulled it from my back pocket, hoping it was Hogany or Money reaching out with good news. Walking off from

Monk Man, I held my breath as I swiped across the screen to check Money's text.

PainInTheAss: My baby a no limit soldier. Everybody can breathe easy now, we in recovery.

The message made me smile and I silently thanked God for looking out once again. I knew I'd be talking to him again soon to repent for the sins I planned to commit next. There was sure to be bodies dropping after the three failed hits.

"Hey, can I talk to you for a second?" Averting my eyes from the phone, I focused my attention on Paris.

"Yeah, we can talk. Where's DJ?"

"Asleep on the couch."

"Okay. We can talk in the kitchen." I gestured for her to walk ahead of me. Entering the kitchen, I leaned up against the sink and waited for her to talk.

"So, look, I'm just gonna be straight up witchu," she started out. "I know I can't undo what happened with Monk Man, but I will try like hell to make it right. I don't know what Derek was thinking. His recklessness is inexcusable and I will be sure to handle it. Monk Man won't have to worry about stepping foot in a courtroom if I can help it."

"I can help it," I said.

"Huh?" She questioned, lost.

"You said Monk Man won't have to worry about stepping foot in a courtroom if you can help it. I'm telling you that *I* can." I knew that my brother wasn't going to be seen in anyone's courtroom the moment he arrived back home from the precinct. Her bd wasn't gonna make it either but under different circumstances.

"Oh, okay." Paris wasn't dumb by a long shot. She knew what the outcome of this situation would be. Even if she didn't know the details of what was to come. She had to know that there was no diplomatic way to handle this.

"Paris, you know how I am when it comes to family, especially my baby brother whom I practically been raising as my own child."

"I understand that and you know I love Monroe just as much. I love you too, Mo." She closed the space between us and used her hands to cup my face. "I can fix this."

"Will your love be the same after I put a bullet in Derek's head?"

She swallowed hard but her eyes never left mine. I wasn't surprised by her reaction nor did I feel a way. In fact, I'd much rather silence than for her to pump fake like she wouldn't care if I killed her child's father. While I had no doubt in my mind that they were strictly co-parenting, the fact was they shared a child.

"Mo, I—."

I covered her hands with mine, removing them from my face. "I'm not mad, P, but you know its family over any and everything. And I'm gon' always cover mine, even if it's at the expense of my own happiness."

<hr>

"I'm confused because I thought I said I wanted everyone that came from my ball sack to be in attendance," my dad grimaced as he walked through my door. Dressed in a Nike Tech sweat-suit and a pair of Uptowns, my dad was as cool as can be. His facial expression though, was anything but cool.

"I know, dad, but Dudas is working a case and Money is at the hospital," I said, closing the door behind him.

"The hell you mean in the hospital. Why is it so much going on with my children that I don't know about? I take it y'all were gonna wait till next Sunday's dinner to fill me in if at all."

I stayed quiet because in all honesty, I didn't plan on telling him anything unless it was absolutely necessary. What I looked like calling him to tell him that I'd dropped the ball? He'd put Monk Man in my care and it was my responsibility to see to it that he was good. Getting caught up in some bullshit that had to do with my relationship wasn't something my father would want to hear.

"Tiffany was shot earlier and Money is at the hospital with her."

"Shit, Mo, why you ain't lead with that over the phone? How she doing?"

"I got a text from Money saying she was out of surgery, so she'll be good." I sighed and rolled my neck to ease some of my tension.

"Where's Monroe?"

"In his room. Let me go get him." I went to walk off but he stopped me.

"Nah. I'll talk to him in a minute. You come and talk to me." We both entered the living room and sat down across from each other. He chose to sit on the loveseat. "When I agreed to let Monk Man stay with you, I didn't make the decision without fully thinking it through. Now, I know with him getting older, some shit he's just gonna have to go through and we can't hold his hand through it all, but getting locked up, Mo. They slapped the cuffs on my boy. Make this shit make sense to me."

"Dad, I'm taking care of it," I assured him. I was still tryna make sense of the shit myself.

"Oh, I have no doubt that you're gonna handle the business. What I'm asking you to do is make this shit make sense *to me*. You ain't been keeping me in the dark, don't start now."

"I got a call from Dudas letting me know that DJ's dad went up to the police station and said that Monk Man has been abusing DJ. Next thing I know, I'm getting a call from Money that the police were here and took him out."

"What's dude's name again?" He asked, standing.

"Derek. I'm taking care of it, dad."

"That makes the two of us. Monroe!" He called out to Monk Man.

"Yeah?" Monk Man responded while making his way up front.

"You coming home with me for a few days." Monk Man's eyes shifted back and forth between me and my dad, lingering on mine a little bit longer. "Ain't no need in looking to her for approval. It's only for a few days. Your sister has work to do. I think she'll operate better without having to worry bout you."

"What about the charge and all dat? Y'all know I ain't hit DJ, right?" His eyes were filled with concern and that pissed me off.

"Hell yeah, we know that. Just go chill out with dad for a few. I'm gonna make some calls and get this all straightened out. You don't have to worry bout nothin', you hear me?"

He nodded. "Yeah, I hear you. Let me go get my stuff."

I leaned in to hug him and whispered in his ear. "Take the company laptop with you." The company laptop was used for The Table business only. It had been designed with a whole bunch of hacker shit that Monk Man requested and was often kept in a safe if it wasn't being used. That's how deep this shit was.

Nodding again, he left the room and headed for his bedroom.

"I'm giving you a few days to have some results, Mo. The only Thompson that knows the inside of the judicial system is Maurice and that was a decision that was out of my hands. Monroe *will not* step foot in a courtroom. This shit shouldn't even live in the air long enough for me to have to get our lawyer involved. If I have to come out of retirement, I'm coming for everything breathing." He kissed my forehead and walked towards the door. "Give Tiff my love and keep me posted."

My father used to be a stone-cold killer back in his day and only those who knew him personally and the ones on the other end of his gun would know that. He used working as a Mason as a front for what he really had going on. The only people in the family who knew about my dad's hidden talent for killing was me, my mother, and Money. He'd done a few jobs for Coolie in his hay day and had a close brotherhood with Tiffany's dad. My dad had long ago passed his guns down to me and Money and I wanted it to stay that way. I knew he had no problem picking them back up if the situation called for it.

"Understood. Consider it taken care of." Monk Man appeared again, this time with a bookbag on his back and a small duffle bag in his hand. "Love you, bro."

"Love you too, sis. Be safe."

"Always."

I walked them out and locked the door behind me thinking, *Derek had no fucking clue how far I was willing to take it behind my loved ones. And if I let my dad loose, it would be like having the grim reaper on your ass.*

Chapter Six

MAHOGANY

The text from Money letting us know that Tiff had pulled through and was in recovery made me shed a tear of relief. Tiff wasn't just my right hand; she was my sister. With both her and Mo by my side, we kept business running and I knew no one would watch my back like them. So, the thought of losing either one of them shook me to my core even though I did my best to hold it together. The image of Tiff laid out on the concrete was an image I was still trying to shake. Someone was at my head with a vengeance, and they were calling me out at every turn. It was time to answer the call.

Before making any moves, I knew I had to go see my godfather. I couldn't text the news of Tiff being shot to her father out of respect. They had a relationship similar to the one I had with my dad. This was news that had to be delivered in person along with my vow to handle the aftermath accordingly. I was relieved to know that I didn't have to come to his door with condolences. My phone rang with an incoming call from Dudas as I whipped Mo's car on the highway.

"I hope you have some good news for me right now cause that's all I wanna hear," I said once the call connected.

"If you look up *luck* in the dictionary, your name and picture should be there for the description," he replied.

"What does that mean, Dudas? I got a whole helluva lot going on right now. I need you to make it plain for me."

"It means that the cameras on the highway where you had your incident are in the process of being upgraded. They were down and other than the few people that reported what they saw tonight, we have nothing to go on. No one was able to make out your license plate or anything."

"And the other car?"

"When EMS and police arrived on scene, the vehicle was still there but no occupants inside. A couple people gave description of your car. I hope—."

"Already taken care of. This ain't amateur night at *the Apollo*."

"Okay, cool. You're in the clear. I'll make sure I keep an ear out in case anything else comes up but it's pretty much an open and shut case. I don't expect that the victim will be coming forward to report anything. I got this shit with Monk Man I gotta handle amongst the other things y'all have subsequently added to my already full plate."

"Yeah, well, add this too. Tiffany was shot not soon after what happened on the highway. It happened in front of Mo's building."

"Fuck! Please tell me she's good." Not only did I pick up on the genuine concern in his tone, but it also held affection and another level of emotion. Deciding not to speak on it, I put it to the back of my mind to address at a later date.

"She's alive and said to fully recover. I have Money at the hospital with her now."

"Damn, okay. Did y'all see or hear anything?"

"Heard gunshots, saw nothing. I was too busy shielding Beautii from everything. I got a call just before the shots rang out, though. I'm gonna send you the number and you see what you can find. Oh, and while you're at it, do me a favor and... you know what, nevermind."

"What, you sure?"

"Yeah. Just look into the number for me."

"Aight, gimmie a few. And I took care of that situation in the projects for you too."

I nodded my head. **"It's good to know that we can always depend on you, Dudas. I just need one more favor."**

"What's that?"

"Make sure you tell your people to make room down at the city morgue. I got a feeling they're gonna be real busy." Hanging up, I dropped my phone inside my purse just as I pulled into Tiff's parents' driveway in Jersey City.

Turning off the ignition, I grabbed my bag from the passenger seat and went to step out of the car when I heard the garage door lift up. Night had settled but with their illuminated driveway, I was able to see Dough standing in the middle of the garage with a big ass gun at his side.

"It's me, Dough," I announced, walking slowly up to the garage entrance so he could see me. As I got closer, I noticed the Ak he toted. This man was crazy as hell. "Really, the Ak 47? Is that the first gun you got your hands on?"

"Something like that. It's late, Hogany," he said, meeting me halfway. "How bad is it and what hospital?"

I wanted to hang my head but to him, it would only show signs of defeat and weakness. And I wasn't waving the red flag nor was I weak.

"She was hit in the chest and she's at Mount Sinai hospital."

"If you're here, who's at the hospital with Tiff?" He questioned, stone faced.

"Money."

He stroked his goatee. "I see. Come inside and give Toni the rundown while I get dressed." My godmother was another person I didn't want to face but I knew the news had to come from me. He went to turn and stopped to face me again. "You know as the head of the head of this shit, everything falls on you, right. Your team is there as support but at the end of the day, everything begins and ends with you."

I heard his words loud and clear, telling me to make shit right and to do so quickly.

IN MAKING THINGS RIGHT, I FOUND MYSELF OUT FRONT OF Santana's hotel after leaving my god parents' house and checking on Beautii. I wasn't a rocket scientist but it didn't take one to put two and two together to make four. It seemed as though my latest problems hadn't started until he touched down in my city. When I mentioned it to Dough, he didn't say that he agreed verbally but he didn't hesitate to give me the address to the hotel Santana and his family were staying in.

Before stepping out of the car, I remembered that I needed to reach out to Briscoe again. The fact that he hadn't picked up the phone for our daughter and we were *in fact* in danger had me ready to go toe to toe with his ass. We'd taken one step forward to go five steps back. Taking out my phone, I went to our text thread and made sure to hit the caps lock button to ensure he got my message loud and clear. He had me fucked up yet again. At this point, he was batting a thousand. As I started to type, something in me told me to look up. When I did, I spotted a man who looked a lot like Santana, walk out of the doors of the Hilton hotel in Midtown.

I followed his movements as his eyes darted East and West before crossing the street. Exiting my messages, I hit the camera icon to record him. He stopped in front of a black Lincoln town car and the driver's side window rolled down. It was clear that the person inside was expecting him. I watched as the backseat window rolled down and the passenger passed a brown paper bag through the window. Quickly checking the contents of the bag, Santana tucked the items tightly under his left arm, bumped fists with the passenger, and stepped back from the car.

I stopped recording, zoomed in on the license plate number, and snapped a picture. *What the fuck is he in to?* I said out loud to myself. Deciding too much had transpired when it came to me and my people within the last 72 hours and given that my daughter had to have a front row to the bullshit, I wasn't going to let the question burn in my head much longer. **BEEP! BEEP!** As he jogged back across the street, I beeped the horn twice, making him snap his head in my direction.

He squinted his eyes and reached for his hip, and I beeped again while rolling my window down at the same time. By the look on his face, I could tell that if he hadn't recognized me, he would have surely flipped.

"If you were about to do something, you sure had me fooled," I said through the open window.

He bopped over to me with a smirk on his face. "To what do I owe this pop-up visit? I thought you wasn't fuckin' with me."

"If this is an indication that I've somehow changed my mind, you must learn how to read the room, Santana," I countered. My tongue was sharper than a double edge sword. "So, you still have friends in New York after all these years, huh?" I subtly made it known that I'd seen the exchange between him and the town car by nodding towards the package he had tucked.

"I do. It's always good to keep your friendships intact. Especially when you have little family."

"I hear you."

"How'd you know where I was staying?"

"Wild guess."

He chuckled and shook his head. "Is that right? Well, you wanna come up? You can meet my girl and my daughter. Or is that too family oriented for you? I wanna respect your boundaries." He held his hands up and I unlocked the car door to get out.

"I'll oblige you this time, but its only because we need to talk business."

"Business?"

"Yeah. Consider this part of your preliminary hearing." I grabbed my bag and after making sure my .380 was snug inside, I hit the key fob to lock the door. "After you."

Smirking again, he switched his package to the left side of his arm and walked ahead of me. *Let the mind games begin*, I said to myself. Santana had *slick* written all over him. It's like I smelled the bullshit from a mile away. My initial plan was to put my people on him to track his movements, but I changed my mind. He needed to know that whatever he thought he was up to, he'd have to work twice as hard to pull the wool over my eyes.

In the elevator, we stood on opposite sides. The moment had a touch of irony because to me, where we currently stood was exactly how I saw us, on opposing teams. The elevator music filled the silence as we rode up to the fourth floor, that was until he decided to speak.

"Dinner was cool. It would've been cool if you would've stayed. You know, ma could've had both of her kids under the same roof after all these years." The elevator stopped and the doors opened. "This us." He held the doors open with his hand and I stepped off first.

"That was a reunion for you and ma and one that y'all needed, not me. How was it seeing your mother after all these years? You know, after you made a choice not to come around."

"You say it like I was just like, fuck my mama. I was a kid when I moved."

"Yeah, and then you grew into a young adult and then a full-grown ass man who made conscious decisions."

"It wasn't a decision I made with the intention to hurt her or you for that matter. I had a lot going on and—."

"There you go again projecting," I cut him off. "Ain't nobody hurt by you not being around, well, I'll speak for myself. I'm sure our mother missed you. I'm not sure what kind of feelings you're trying to evoke from me."

He snickered. "Man, you ain't gon' let me forget that you don't fuck with me, huh?"

"If I were you, I wouldn't take it personal. I'm like this with all the niggas I don't know. I've seen that overly friendly, overly welcoming shit get niggas double crossed and sometimes killed." My words were well thought out.

"I ain't no random ass nigga though, I'm yo' brother."

"That something you feel the need to keep reminding me of?" I threw his shit back at him with a twist.

With a slight smile, he shook his head. "Touché. Lemme ask you a question, though. This whole tough girl thing you got going on, you put that body armor on before you leave the house every morning?" He swiped his keycard and pushed the door open to his hotel room.

"Bae?" I heard a female call out who I assumed was his girl.

"Who else would be opening the door with a key, baby?" He questioned and gestured with his head for me to come inside. I chose not to answer the tough girl question because I woke up a *real bitch* on the daily and went to sleep the same way.

"I'm just making...oh shoot, I didn't know we were having company." She closed her robe but not before I caught an eyeful of her nakedness. "I'm sorry bout that," she said, tying the robe tight and using her hands to hold the belt. "You could've warned me that your sister was witchu, bae, dang."

"In his defense, he didn't know I was coming," I spoke up. "You good though. I'm quite fond of my own pussy so the image of yours will not be one I commit to memory."

Her brows raised in surprise at my response. "Ummm, lemme go throw something on." She left the room quickly.

"That's my lady, Renee," Santana said casually. "My daughter in the room probably glued to her phone. Let me go get her." He walked off and I made myself comfortable at the kitchenette.

I took a moment to look around the hotel and concluded that Santana was either modest or he wasn't touching no big paper. I didn't have certain expectations, but after seeing how he had his family put up, I could understand why he wanted to fuck with a big dawg such as myself. He reappeared with his girl who was now fully dressed in leggings and an oversized t-shirt. Renee was a pretty girl and seeing how innocent she appeared, I wouldn't have paired her with Santana.

"Asia in there knocked out. It may have been that food that your mother made. She threw down," Renee spoke.

"Yea, she can burn," I agreed.

"Where yo' lil' one at?" Santana asked. "Y'all made it home? I know you mentioned being tired." Hearing him mention me making it home made my ears ring.

"Funny you should ask that. We actually never made it home. Some crazy bastard tried to run me and my kid off the road."

"Oh my God, what?!" Renee exclaimed. "Is she okay? Where is she?"

"She's good, with family."

"That shit is crazy. Where dat happen at and why you so calm about it?" Santana spoke up and his reaction was just as shocked as his girl's.

"That's neither here nor there, we came out unscathed. This part gon' take you out though. My sister was shot right in front of my daughter not even an hour after this incident. I mean, y'all have a little girl of your own so you can only imagine how I'm feeling after mine had to witness all this shit in one night." In a smooth transition, I pulled the .380 from my bag and sat it on the table within arm's reach.

"Ohh, I see what this is." Santana wagged his finger in my direction while Renee took cover behind him. "If you think I had something to do with that shit, just be straight up and ask."

"Okay," I stood, cocked the gun back, and pointed it directly at the duo. "Did you have anything to do with what went on tonight or the shooting at my club? I'm finding it hard to believe that you and your family show up in my city and coincidentally all hell start breaking loose. Now, I'm not a stranger to beef but at my level, that's small-scale shit. What's going on at the moment is a motherfucka gunning straight for my head. And that shit don't sit well with me. You can understand that, right?"

His face turned up, showing he'd taken direct offense to what I had implied. "First off, the fact that you up in my shit pointing guns and making accusations is disrespect on a whole other level. Secondly, I don't know what made you think a nigga can't get on the same shit you on." A once seemingly scared Renee stepped from behind Santana, with a gun in her hand that she upped on me. "Third, I ain't have nothing to do with none of that shit."

"Hmmm, let me guess, I should believe that because we're family, right?" I purposely ignored Renee by not even glancing in her direction when I spoke.

"Shit, I ain't tryna convince you but fuck I look like tryna kill you? I already told you I'm tryna do business."

Running my tongue across my teeth, I lowered my gun and picked up my purse. "Thanks for having me."

"Wait, hol' up, time out," Santana let out. "What kinda shit you on?"

"You passed the first level of your preliminary screening, Santana. I'll be in touch with an address, and we can clear you for level two. Oh, and

Renee, you gon' have to let one off to make me believe you bout that shit next time, mami."

See the difference between me and most was I was a plotting ass bitch. Leaving their hotel room, I knew I'd left a lasting impression. Now, time would have to tell if I was right about Mr. Santana Coast.

Chapter Seven

SANTANA

"I'm not feelin' this shit, Santana. I'm not feelin' this shit at all," Renee expressed with the gun she'd pulled from my waistband at her side. I could only chuckle, completely tripped out by what had just gone down. "This shit ain't funny, Santana!" She shoved me and handed me the gun.

"I know, bae. Shit, I'm just as lost as you. Ion know what that shit was about. You did what you was supposed to do, though." I leaned in to kiss her and she dodged my lips.

"No. I don't wanna kiss right now. This isn't a game! Did you forget our daughter was in the next room? She knew that and still pulled a gun out on us. What if she would've let a shot off, Santana?!"

"If she wanted to shoot, she would've. Chill out with all the dramatic shit." Tucking my gun back in my jeans, I remembered the package I had in my arm. Leaving Renee steaming in the living room, I headed for our temporary bedroom. She wasn't far behind.

"How did she even know we were staying at this hotel? Did you have anything to do with her being ran off the road?"

"Hell no! Why would I do that shit knowing she got her kid in the car?" I sat down on the edge of the bed, and she cut her eye at me with her arms folded tightly across her chest. "What, you think I'm lying?" Now I was offended.

"I'm not saying that. But don't act like you're above doing some reckless shit. Remember, I've been on some of those reckless missions with you." I knew what she was hinting at, but I'd long ago buried that incident way back in my mind in order to sleep at night.

"Yeah, well, this ain't that and I ain't do that shit." Pulling out the contents of the brown paper bag, I sat it down on the bed. Tightly sealed in saran wrap was a ki of coke. I marveled at how the brick sparkled through the packaging.

"Santana, what are we doing here? And this time, be straight up with me because now I'm starting to feel like you haven't been. Blood sister or not, ain't no way you just let someone pull a gun out on us and walk outta here like shit is all gravy. Then you pull that shit out of a bag like a magic trick." She pointed at the brick, seeking answers.

"We fucked up," I let out.

"Fucked up how?"

"Our pockets, bae. I just spent the last of what I had saved up on this work." Saying that shit out loud left a bitter taste in my mouth.

"Bae, why didn't you say anything before we came here?" She sat down next to me and rubbed the back of my neck. "We supposed to move as one, Santana. Nothing has changed. And you know I always got you so you can have us."

"I know, baby. A nigga just feel like less than and figured I could make something shake before you noticed what was going on." I heard her sigh before clasping her hand in mine.

"What we need to do?" I didn't expect any other response from her. Renee had put in the time and proven that she was down for me time and time again. This time around would be no different.

"Shit, we got nothing but opportunity here on the East Coast. It's a fully operated business that's mine for the taking. You know I love the West Coast, but this is where we need to be."

"So, you saying you wanna move out here permanently?"

"I'm saying in order to get the reward, we gotta take big risk. And it won't hurt for us to have a change of scenery. This business at The Table is big, baby. I'm gon' get that seat and we gon' be living better than we ever have."

"And what about my job? Asia just started cheerleading at school and she has all of her friends back home. This is a big decision, bae."

"I know, and one I don't take lightly. You know I ain't gon' steer us wrong tho. The boat may rock along the journey but we ain't sinking. You just gotta trust yo' man. The plans are already in motion. And I have a way to get in good with Mahogany."

She sighed. "Alright, Santana. You're the head of this family. I just hope that this don't come back to bite us in the ass."

"Come here." I pulled her up and sat her down on my lap. "I got us, bae. Just give me a little bit of time and we gon' be straight. I'm sure we can get you plugged in wit' a job here. I'll check wit' my mom's regarding school for Asia."

"Uh huh."

Grabbing her chin, I pulled her face down to kiss her lips. "You're all I got, Renee."

"And all you'll ever need," she responded with conviction and covered my lips with hers. I had her buy in at 100%.

I WATCHED RENEE SLEEP PEACEFULLY, CURLED UP IN A FETAL position after I'd given her some dick full of reassurance. I wanted her fully on board with this move to New York and I was confident that I had erased any doubts she may have had. Truth was, I'd made all that shit up about us being fucked up. We were straight on money. I had a nice little nest egg that could hold us over for a minute but that wasn't enough for me. As I stated before, I wanted it *all* and I was gonna have it.

Mahogany didn't know it yet, but she'd given me my way in, and I was gonna work it to my advantage. I truly didn't know shit about her getting ran off the highway or her girl getting hit up. Sis had enemies lurking in the shadows and it just further showed that she wasn't cut out for this game. To have no clue who was at her top and for the people in her camp to be just as clueless was a no no. And that's where I'd come in; big brother to save the day.

I'd find someone or better yet have Razor find someone to put the club shooting on and clap they ass to show that I was in her corner. That wouldn't be hard seeing as the cousin of the actual shooter was in the wind with the getaway car used in the shooting. Razor was on the case, so I was depending on him to come through. Even if I had to pull on some of my resources to get what I needed, I would see to it that the job was done.

Using my resources was how I'd managed to get the brick that sat inside of the hotel dresser for next to nothing. I'd reached out to my guy Snake who owed me big, and he'd given me the work for the low. The plan was to get it to Razor, have him break it down, and sack it up. I had to put something in his hands to move or he'd be on the first flight back to L.A. I couldn't have that. He was my only ally at the moment.

The ball was still in Mahogany's court although she'd checked it when she popped up on me. By the way she drew on me and Renee out of nowhere, it seemed to me that the stress of the unknown was starting to get to her. The more wound up and erratic she became, she was bound to start slipping up. That would then make Coolie reevaluate her position as head of The Table, subsequently resulting in him handing me the position. Then, *I'd* be the man.

At this point, my plans were playing out before I got a chance to make a move. Maybe I needed to look into finding out who else was at her head. I had a feeling that we'd be an asset to each other. With thoughts of my next meet up with Mahogany for part two of my "preliminary hearing," I snuggled up behind Renee.

Kissing her neck, I whispered in her ear. "Sleep well my baby. Daddy bout to see to it that you never have to work again. I'm bout to be King round this bitch."

Chapter Eight

TIFFANY

"I'm saying tho, she looks uncomfortable in this little ass bed. Y'all don't have a queen size tempur pedic or something? How she supposed to heal if she's uncomfortable?"

I could hear Money fussing with someone for the second time today and I knew whoever the person was, they were over his ass. It didn't matter that his request was unreasonable, he wasn't letting up. The first time I thought it was a dream until my eyes fluttered open and I heard the loud beeping sounds of hospital machines. I knew where I was before I opened my eyes, and I knew how I got here. I was also anxious to get out.

"Sir, you do know that this is a hospital and not a hotel, right?" The woman's response was spicy, and I was tickled because I just knew he was bout to get on her ass and there was nothing anyone could do to save her.

"Miss, I'm not into disrespecting women but I'll violate a bitch. Go head and get someone above you before I have a couple of my cousins from the Westside come see bout you."

I couldn't see the woman's face with him standing in front of her, but I did hear her gasp followed by the door closing. She had to be white too because only white women did that dramatic ass shit. A black woman would've put it all on the line and cussed his ass smooth out.

"Why you keep giving these people a hard time, Montez?" I finally spoke. "I don't need another bed. What I need is to get up outta here and find out who did this shit." I wanted to sit up straight but if the burning in my chest from lying flat was any indication of what I'd feel sitting up on my own, I could wait.

"I ain't giving nobody a hard time. I'm just simply making sure my lady straight. I knew yo ass was over there faking sleep too." He made his way over to me and helped get me in a comfortable position. Fluffing my pillow, he used the remote to sit the bed up a little. "Better?" He asked, pecking my forehead.

"Yes, thank you." Today was my second day in the hospital and he hadn't left my side. He was so gentle and attentive and had even survived my dad.

They'd been in each other's presence on many occasions but had never said more than a few words to each other. According to him, when my parents came by, I was still out of it from the surgery where they pulled the bullet out of my chest. Mahogany had pulled some strings so that they were able to see me after visiting hours. I was glad to hear that she was able to pull something off because knowing my dad, wouldn't nobody be able to stop him from seeing me. Hospital protocol be damned.

Money said when my dad walked into my room, he didn't say two words, just made a beeline to me. He stood back while my dad did his own assessment of my wound and my mother rubbed my head softly, assuring me that I was gonna be good. The doctors had me under heavy sedation, so I didn't recall the interaction at all. They stayed for a while and at some point, my dad pulled Money to the side. He refused to tell me what they talked about. All he said was my dad was solid, something I already knew.

"I want you to be comfortable. You've been laying here stiff as a bitch."

"Nigga, I just got shot, ain't that many positions I can lay in. And ain't nobody faking sleep. The doctor said I need my rest, remember," I retorted as if I planned to take the advice. Two days had been long enough, and I knew I'd heal better at home.

"Yeah, I do. And then you told her you'll rest when you die."

"Exactly. I'm only staying one more day, if that, then we gotta wrap this shit up. I can't find the bitch behind this if I'm laid up in here." Turning my head, I closed my eyes. I wasn't tired but I needed to center myself.

My eyes were closed only a few seconds before I felt the right side of the bed shift. Before I could say anything to Money, he spoke first.

"On some real shit, ma, you had a nigga scared ta death. And though I never counted you out, seeing you on that ground did something to me. You're the only other woman I hold close to my heart outside of my sister and Mahogany. Don't try to hit me with that, *we ain't together* bs either. You know I don't care about nunna dat hot shit you be spittin'. We one round this bitch."

The conviction coupled with the fact that I knew he was genuine made me swallow any smart remark I did have. Little did Money know, me being combative with him was my way of keeping my feelings for him at bay. However, him being by my side and being the first face I saw when I woke up made my heart flutter. The love Money and I had for each other was complicated. And while he had no problems expressing his feelings out loud, I kept mine reserved and expressed them inwardly.

"Montez..." I went to speak and was interrupted by the parade that entered my room, led by my Goddy.

"They said there was a gangsta down and I just had to come see for myself," Goddy said, walking over to me with pink roses from Venus ET Fleur. My face lit up because I loved flowers. "I got you a small arrangement cause you ain't gon' be here long, boo. I had to stop they ass from coming in here with balloons and shit." She pointed behind her at Mahogany, Mo, and Beautii. "That shit is for people with an extended stay, and we don't need you getting comfortable up in here."

"Thank you, Goddy. I love them. And yes, you know I'm ready to blow this joint." She came around to hug me and kiss my cheek.

"We'll talk later, shorty." Money gave my thigh a light squeeze and got up to give the ladies space. "I'm gonna run out real quick. Y'all want anything from the store?"

"Oooh, can you get me a chop cheese on a hero, lightly toasted bread, Uncle Money?" All eyes went to Beautii who had no issue rattling off her order.

"You hungry, Beautii girl?" I asked while chuckling. "I don't think they do chop cheese on this side of town."

"She ain't hungry, she greedy," Hogany let out.

"Eat like she got a damn tape worm," Goddy second.

"Don't trip, niece," Money said. "If I can't find that, I'll get you something close to it. You want anything, bae?" He asked me.

"Yeah, bae," Mo teased, "you want anything?"

"Shut up. And no, thank you."

"Cool. Text me if you change your mind." He left out again and the foursome took a spot on my hospital bed.

There was barely any room on the small bed, but I was fine with having them close. Especially after almost being a memory.

"I swear he reminds me so much of Coolie," Goddy said. "He's so attentive and you just be igging his ass, just like I used to do Coolie in the beginning." She gushed as she always did when she spoke my godfather's name.

"Ma, please. You weren't playing hard to get on the level she do," Mahogany chimed in.

"Uhhh, *she* is right here," I let out.

"I know," Mahogany snickered. "How you feeling though, boo? You don't look like you been in a shootout."

"Yeah, well I feel like it. For the most part I'm okay, just really sore. I guess whatever meds they got going through this I.V. must be working. I'm ready to get the hell outta here, though."

"I don't see why they can't discharge you today. You got a man ready to wait on you hand, foot, and..." Mo stopped talking and eyed Beautii. Mahogany cleared her throat and nodded towards the door.

"Dang, I even get kicked out of the hospital room? That's crazy." Beautii shook her head and leaned over to hug me, careful to avoid hurting me. "I'm glad you're okay, Aunty Tiff. I love you."

"I love you, too, Beautii girl." She kissed my cheek and left out with Goddy.

"Okay, give me the rundown on what's really going on," I said, snapping into business mode quick.

Mo glanced over at Mahogany then back at me.

"What?" I pushed.

"Tell her, Hogany," Mo egged on. "Tell her about the latest move."

"I'm thinking about pulling Coast in," she said.

"Your brother?"

"My mother's son, yes."

"Bitch, you need to kill that," I said. "He's your brother and you just don't fuck with him and that's understandable. That said, if you don't even wanna fuck with him on a personal level, and blood relatives is as personal as it gets, why bring him into the business?"

"That's what I said," Mo agreed.

"I hear and understand y'all concerns. At the same time, y'all know I'm never gonna move without having fully thought a plan through. I gotta keep this dude close. I have this nagging feeling that all this bullshit that's gone down is somehow tied to him. If he ain't making the plays, then someone else is pulling the strings. Either way, I want him under my thumb."

"Well, while he's under your thumb, I'ma have the beam on his head. If that nigga even breathe funny, I'ma rearrange his facial structure," Mo made clear. "I'm tired of playing with these motherfuckas."

"Straight like that," I concurred. "Now, I've been in this hospital for two days, please tell me y'all got some kind of lead of the fucker that shot me." My lip curled up just thinking about someone else having one up on us.

"So far, nothing. I had Dudas track the number that called me before the shots rang out. The number was traced back to a burner phone."

"Damn."

"Yeah. We'll figure this shit out soon enough, though. We don't have a choice but to. Niggas not about to be walking around telling stories that include us being on the other side of the gun."

"Right." Mo nodded. "I'ma bout to narrow down the suspect pool soon as I leave here too."

"Lemme guess, you going to see Paris' bd."

"I am. As a matter of fact, let me head that way now. I love you and I'm glad you're good." She gave me a hug and stood to do the same with Hogany. "I'm gonna check on the traps and make sure things are good before I make my move."

"Okay. Mo, remember those bullshit charges are still up in the air. We need him alive to drop them," Mahogany let her know.

"Work his ass, not too bad, and don't kill him, got it." She left and I shook my head.

"When can I check myself out?" I asked her.

"Tomorrow morning. Dudas just needs to stop by and put on record that he interviewed you. You know we gotta make it look good."

"Cool, cause I am ret ta go." Silence fell over the room and Hogany pulled at the loose string on the hospital sheet. "Hogany."

"Yeah?"

"You know this shit comes with the territory, right."

"Yeah, I know. I also know that as the head of this shit, I'm responsible for the body. Somebody is at my head, Tiff. And because of that, you got hit with a bullet that we both know was meant for me."

"And now that you've laid out the facts as you see them, let's get to the solution. We're The Table, Hogany. We gon' get our lick back and we gon' keep it moving with the expansion. You know a nigga gotta answer for this." I pointed at my chest wound.

"I don't see no way around it, gangsta." I held my hand out for her to take.

I had someone I'd thrown in the suspect pool myself and I planned to pay them a visit once I was released. It would rain bullets in the city before I was able to sleep peacefully knowing someone had a bullet with my name on it.

Chapter Nine

MORAE

At Mahogany's request, I sat with my thoughts for two days before making a move on Paris' bd. Unfortunately, for him, that was two days of me coming up with different ways to fuck his life up without doing direct harm to him. Now, I wasn't stupid, I knew he needed to be unharmed in order to get the charges against Monk Man dropped. I was gonna give him a lot to think about though. His ass was sure to be running to that courthouse to drop them charges.

While everything played out, I told Monk Man to go about life as usual. I wasn't keeping him out of school, and he wasn't about to be moving like he had a case over his head. When I said I was going to take care of something, it was as good as done. He knew that he could count on me and assured me that he wasn't worried. And that's what I wanted to hear.

Before I could handle personal business, I wanted to tap in with the lieutenants. We needed to ensure that business was running as usual. Normally, I'd check in via phone but with all that had been going on, I felt that a face-to-face pop up was fitting. Mahogany may have been confident that we didn't have to worry about anyone in our camp, but I still wanted to make sure that we operated on a system of checks and balances. It was best to be leery of any and every one until we found the culprit.

I pulled up on Pete first since I was closer in distance to him. Dialing his number as I parked across the street from the brownstone in Manhattan that he used as the main hub for his traps, a text came through from Paris. It was the first time she'd reached out to me since leaving my place two days ago. Knowing the timing I was on, I ignored the message and continued with my call. The phone rang three times before he picked up.

"What's the word, Mo?"

"I'm outside of your spot. Come talk to me for a minute." I moved my purse from the passenger seat and put it in the back to make room for him.

"You just missed me. I had to run out and take care of something."

"Funny, I just got word that your truck was out front." Pete had a chauffeur who doubled as his security that drove him around in his black Denali truck. The same truck that was parked in front of the building.

"I have more than one means of transportation, Mo. I would think it wise to do so given the business we're in, don't you think?"

"I see your logic," I responded, already concluding that he was moving funny.

"Usually when someone wants to see me, they call first. That way it saves them a trip in case I'm not around."

"Yeah, well, today, I didn't feel like playing telegram, Pete. More often than not, I'm gonna pop up should I feel the need to."

"And I may be out," he countered.

"Noted. I'll get with you at another time."

"I..." I'd already killed the line. I had nothing else to talk to him about, especially after sensing deceit.

It didn't help that Mahogany had done a pull up in Pete's neck of the woods and the shooting at the club happened not too soon after. One would think that he would want to move in a way where he wasn't on our radar. This stunt he pulled today put him right in my line of sight. And it wasn't so much as us wanting to control the movements of the people on our team, but Pete's responses made me want to pick apart his story.

Putting my car in drive, I prepared to pull off when I spotted his driver exiting the lower level of the brownstone. *"Ain't this a bitch,"* I said out loud. I knew that if the driver was around, Pete was nearby. Shifting back into park, I watched the driver scan the block, then head back inside; odd. It was a good thing I'd switched cars today and rode lowkey in my X5. Like my other cars, my windows were tinted so while I could see the driver, I was sure he wouldn't have noticed me if he'd passed the car.

A few minutes went by, and I waited patiently knowing some bullshit was amiss. And just as I predicted, Pete emerged from the brownstone the same way the driver had. I could see him clear as day as his eyes darted up and down the street before moving towards the truck. His driver opened the back door and for a moment, Pete looked across the street and stared for a few seconds. I stared back as if he could see me, hoping he somehow felt my presence. Putting his phone to his ear, he hopped in the backseat.

Saying fuck it in my head, I put my hand on the door handle and started to get out but thought of a better idea. Seeing that he felt the need to lie about being around, I knew it would be hard to convince me that he wasn't flawed. The Denali started up and I shifted my car into drive to follow it. As the truck pulled off smoothly, my phone rang. Using the car's Bluetooth to connect the call, I let two cars drive ahead of me and fell in line behind them to tail the Denali.

"Hello," I spoke.

"I have your package. Do you want it inside the house, or should I set it up in the garage?"

"The garage is fine, thank you."

"Cool. You need me to stay with it?"

I paused to make a right along with the Denali and the two cars that aided in my tail. **"Yeah. It won't be for long, though."** The line beeped with an incoming call from Hogany. **"Let me get this. You know what to do if you have any issues with set up, right."**

"Yep. Send the package back to the manufacturer."

"Exactly. I'll be in touch." I clicked over at the same time the car in front of me turned the corner, leaving one car in between me and the Denali. **"Everything good?"** I asked Hogany once the call connected.

"Where you at?" She questioned.

"If I told you, you wouldn't believe me."

"Try me."

"I'm tailing, Pete."

"Why wouldn't I believe that?" The fact that she hadn't asked me why made me alert.

"That wasn't the response I expected."

"Shit, I didn't expect to find out Pete's ass was a snake, but you know God works in mysterious ways."

"Do tell," I pried, wanting to know what she'd found out.

"Let's just say that Pete is kin to a mouse whom I had the displeasure of coming in contact with and exterminating."

I thought about what she said, and the lightbulb went off in my head. **"Dude from the projects."**

"He's Pete's godson."

"Oh, this shit just gets better and better. You think he know about your dad? Better yet, do you think he had anything to do with the set up?"

"Highly likely. What direction is he headed?"

"Looks like he pulling up in front of the Hilton in Midtown. I parked on the corner. He just got out." I could see Pete step out of the truck, exchange a few words with his driver, and bop across the street to the hotel entrance. **"What you want me to do?"** I asked, pulling the P365 from under my seat and placing it on my lap.

"Stand down and drop your location. I'll get someone on it."

"Copy."

"Oh, and don't worry about checking in with the other lieutenants. I'm gonna have Money on it. You go head and settle up with Derek. We need to put this situation with Monk Man to bed before the fire gets bigger."

"Heard." Hanging up, I drove slowly down the street and pass the Denali. Niggas were up to no good and the rabbit hole was getting deeper and deeper.

I arrived at the used car lot/mechanic shop where Derek worked and made sure that both of my guns were locked and loaded before stepping out of my car. The P365 rested at the bottom of my bag and my Beretta tucked in my waist. Dressed casually in a pair of fitted cargo pants, a Diesel hoodie, and a pair of Rick Owens sneakers, it didn't appear that I was looking for confrontation. Oh, but I was. And I was prepared to lay down anything moving funny.

Entering the gate, I navigated through the slew of broke down cars which stood out more than the ones that were marked for sale. Derek had no clue that I knew where he worked. Hell, I knew everything about his ass, down to the hospital he was born in. In my line of work, it was important to not only know about your inner circle but those they were attached to as well. I learned that from my dad a long time ago.

"Hey, can I help you?" A short, chubby looking Mexican with a round face and spiked hair asked. He must've liked what he saw because he stood before me, licking his lips and wiping what I was sure was motor oil off his stubby hands.

"Is Derek in?"

He gave me a once over and nodded towards the back. "He's back there with his lady friend. You wanna go back? The door is open." His little ugly ass was tryna be messy, but little did he know, this wasn't a social visit.

"Just point me in the direction and I'll find my way." He pointed to the back, and I took note of the door with the *office* sign on it. Before heading that way, I dug into my bag and pulled out a hundred-dollar bill. "Whatever you hear in that office, you be sure to keep your mouth shut and go about your day as normal, entiendes?"

"No problem," he replied and nodded, pocketing the C-note.

"Hey, does this place have cameras?"

"Yeah, but they don't work. The owner is a cheap ass."

"Thanks."

I proceeded to walk to the back and as I got closer to the office, I could clearly hear Paris' voice.

"You need to drop those charges, Derek. Your issue is with me, it has nothing to do with anyone else," she argued. The stress in her tone could've been taken for some kind of plea.

"This shit got everything to do with that carpet munching ass bitch you with!" Derek spat. "And I ain't droppin' shit. You lucky I don't come over there and beat that lil' nigga's ass for putting his hands on my son."

"Oh, please. You know damn well her brother didn't lay a hand on DJ. DJ told me himself that you pushed him, and he fell into the couch. Yo bitch ass is the one that needs to be brought up on charges because you can't control your fucking temper! Unlike you, I don't play cop games."

"Oh, so you gangsta now cause you with the dyke, huh?"

"Get the fuck out my face, Derek."

"Or what? What you gon' do, Paris, getcho ass whipped like you used to?"

Yeah, this pussy had the game fucked up. Me and Paris may have been in a weird space but ain't no way I was gon' stand by and let a nigga threaten her. That on top of threatening bodily harm to my brother was a violation. Using my sleeve, I twisted the doorknob and pushed the door open. Four eyes were now on me, with Paris showing fear and uncertainty. She took a step back from Derek and a step towards me.

"Looks like we have ourselves a little reunion," Derek said snidely and turned so that he was fully facing me.

"Yeah, I guess we do, but not a *friendly* one." Pulling my gun from my waistband, I pointed directly at his head. Out the corner of my eye, I could see Paris flinch while Derek did his best to maintain his tough guy persona.

He snickered. "There are cameras all around this place, bitch. You can shoot me if you want. It'll only land you in the place your brother will be shortly."

POP! POP! Before he knew what was happening, I let off two shots, hitting the wall, shattering a picture of Mohammed Ali. He jumped out of my line of fire real quick.

"Are you fucking crazy?!"

"Mo," Paris called my name, and I gave her a quick glance, letting her know to stand down.

"Crazy? No," I answered Derek. "But insane? Yes. Derek, the last thing I want you to think is that I'm the bitch to be fucked with, cause thinking that will prove to be dangerous to not only your health but those you love and associate with. I'm willing to go to jail and play in hell about the people I love, understand that. That was the only warning shot I'll be letting off in this bitch. Now, those fraudulent ass charges you have against my brother, you're going to drop today. If not," I shrugged my shoulders, "well, your mother's blood will be on your hands."

"Bitch...what!" He took a step in my direction with his fist balled and I let off another shot. This time, it grazed his ear. He reached up to grab it and pulled his hand back to examine it.

"Something tells me you're not hearing me." Walking up on him, every bit of my 5'7" frame stood under his 5'9" height. What he had on me in height, had nothing on what I had on him in balls. I placed the barrel of the gun to his neck. I knew he could feel the heat from the gun by the hissing sound he made, as it was still hot from the shots I'd let off. "Someone will be here in thirty minutes to escort you down to the precinct to get that done. Make no mistake about it, you can either bury your mother or she can bury you after I torch this bitch with you and that greasy fucker out front in it. And trust me when I say this is far from a threat. This is a **promise**. You got thirty minutes to getcho ass in gear." I spoke through clenched teeth, pushing the barrel further into his neck.

Up close, I could see the fear in his eyes. Yes, I was a woman, small in stature, but the gun in his was face was a sign of the severity of the situation at hand. Pulling the gun back, I turned to leave not the least bit concerned with him coming at me from behind. With no words spoken, Paris followed. As we exited the office, I locked eyes with the Mexican guy who nodded his head and went back to his work.

Outside, I texted my contact the address to the shop and told them to arrive in the thirty-minute time frame I'd given Derek. I also texted Dudas that the situation was being handled and to let me know if the deed was done. I wasn't letting Derek's mother go until I saw the proof in black and white. And the turnaround time would determine whether she was returned to him battered and bruised or in the pristine condition we'd found her. To put a little fire under his ass, I had the handler I'd tasked to watching her, send a picture of her to Derek's phone. This shit was far from a game.

"Morae, you don't hear me calling you?" Paris asked from beside me.

"Wassup?"

"What the hell was that back there?"

"Go home, Paris," was the only answer I provided. I kept moving to my car, only for her to follow behind me.

"No, Morae. Do you wanna go to fucking jail?" She snatched me by my arm, and I spun around. "Look at what he's trying to do to Monroe. Do you think he'll have a problem doing the same with you? What the hell were you thinking? I was handling it."

I looked down at my arm then back up at her. "Why you never told me that nigga was going upside your head?" Silence. "I'm thinking you need to get in your car and go home, Paris." My tone was even but the demand was evident. "This shit is happening whether you want to believe it or not." If she wanted to stick around for the aftermath, she could but I had done what I came to do.

I left out of the lot and walked across the street to my car. Starting the car up, I watched Paris stomp off to her car, get in, and peel out. I dialed my handler as I watched her car disappear down the clock.

"**Yo,**" he answered.

"**If you don't get a call from me within the next two hours, make it clean and quick.**"

"**Understood.**" I ended the call and drove off.

Derek could play like he wasn't gonna comply if he wanted to and live to regret that he ever crossed paths with me.

Chapter Ten

JUSTICE

I SAT IN MY STUDY WITH 50 CENTS "MANY MEN" PLAYING low on my surround sound system. A slew of papers lay sprawled out on my desk and my mind was in overdrive trying to piece together a puzzle. I'd been at it for the last few hours and felt a breakthrough coming somewhere. Picking up a file with one hand and a cup of green tea with the other, I heard a knock at the door.

"Come in," I said, not bothering to look up from the file. Only one other person resided in the house with me and that was my mother. The door was pushed open, and she entered the room.

"Hey, son. How's everything?" The smell of her Caroline Herrera perfume reached me before she did. Making her way over, she took a seat in the chair, in front of my desk.

"I can't call it, ma. I'm still tryna piece this shit together. I could use another set of eyes."

"And how bout a listening ear? You got that look on your face. The one that daddy used to have when he had more on his mind than he cared to share."

Standing, she leaned over the desk to look over the papers with me.

"Shit, other than this right here," I pointed to the desk, "I'm having a hard time taking your advice when it comes to this Mahogany situation."

"I see. Well, son, I haven't advised you on anything that you don't already know. You're close enough to the situation as it is. How do you think he's gonna take it that the man he hired to be *the fixer* is courting his daughter?"

Her question was valid and one that had crossed my mind many times. I didn't expect things to play out the way they had thus far, and now it was up to me to figure out how to navigate this shit without it getting messy. The question floated around in my head as I thought about my visit to an old friend of the family a couple months ago.

Entering San Quentin prison, I went through all the necessary check points and the extra shit before getting to the visiting room. I wasn't a fan of prisons, or the penal system as a whole, for that matter. And for that reason, I made sure to stay from around people who seemed to attract both. This wasn't the case with the person I was here to see today. This was a requested visit by a close family friend who I hadn't seen since my father's funeral five years ago.

I knew that if this man was requesting my presence, then he had a need that only I could fulfill. On top of that, he'd reached out to my mother personally and she encouraged the visit.

After being seated, myself along with the other visitors waited another few minutes before the inmates filed in. One by one, the orange jumpsuits entered the visiting room, each man heading to their assigned tables to greet their families. While they appeared happy in the moment, I knew that sinking feeling knowing that the two-hour visit was the closest thing they'd have to normalcy ate at them. It was the very reason why I vowed to never even make this place a pit stop throughout my years in the underworld.

The last inmate to pass through the steel doors was Curtis "Coolie" Wright himself. The man still managed to have an air of confidence about himself as if he were walking the gritty streets of New York, where he hailed from Harlem to be exact.

"Jus, what's going on, gangsta?" He greeted and we embraced in a manly hug.

"Living life, man. You know me." He nodded and sat down across

from me. "You know this ain't my scene, but I figured if you reached out, it was imperative that I make the trip. How can I be of assistance?"

"I appreciate that. You know I'm not one for beating around the bush. I have five names for you. Five people who need to disappear. I need it discreet and quiet. Now, I could put my people on it, but this matter requires a certain amount of sophistication and skill that only a Blackstone possesses."

I smiled because it was rare that you heard a man in Coolie's position put respect on another man's name. Coolie was a timeless gangsta. Just like my old man before he passed. It was the reason that they were able to maintain a solid friendship despite the rocky way it started out.

"They have anything to do with the reason you in here?" I asked.

"**Everything** to do with it."

"Say less. What's the number?" I asked the price he wanted to pay for the task he'd put before me.

"100k. Twenty bands for each. I'll have Dough do all of the recon and get the intel over to you."

"You sure Dough won't get the urge to take care of the business himself?" I smirked and he laughed.

"I'll make sure that he doesn't. Besides, it's not Dough I'd have to worry about. It'll be my daughter."

I nodded. "Well, you know I need access to your case files too, right? Once I get what's needed, consider it done. You know where to wire the money to."

"Offshore, family business account?"

"Correct."

"It'll be there in the next 24hours. How's your mom?"

"She's good. How's the family?"

"Staying strong in my absence. You know I have my daughter, Mahogany, out there holding it down for me."

"Oh yeah? How's that going?" I'd never met Coolie's daughter before but to know that he had placed his organization in her hands during his timeout spoke volumes.

"She's handling the business. Making her old man proud." He smiled like a proud dad. "Every day she proves to me that I made a smart move putting her in position."

"That's wassup. If it's cool witchu, I'ma get ready to skate." I stood and he did the same. We gave each other a solid handshake and half hug.

"Three months," he asked for confirmation.

"It's already done."

And now here I was going through both Coolie's case and the remaining intel I'd received from Dough. All the while, trying to shake Mahogany from my thoughts. I hadn't spoken to her since the night she'd asked me about the Dodge Charger. The question was so random, I had to laugh. Her rushing me off the phone and the fact that I hadn't heard from her since was bothering me.

"So, why does this person have an X on the picture?" My mother questioned, holding a photo up of a guy named Yasir. I refocused and looked at the picture she held in her hand.

I smirked. "Mahogany took care of him. Granted, it wasn't discreet like her dad would have liked it. In fact, it was *very loud*, but Ms. Mahogany still walks amongst us a free woman."

My mother nodded and smiled. "Her people have her covered. I like her already. My question still remains the same, though."

"Ma, you and I both know that Coolie knows we've come in contact. That man don't have his daughter out here naked." I spoke while picking up different photos and separating them by remaining victims. I already had a plan in motion to kill the remaining four birds with one stone using the one thing that made the world go round, money.

"Is it worth it?" She pried. I'd absentmindedly put my hand up to my chest where I'd been shot and she picked up on it. "I assume you feel that it is."

The night I took the bullet for Mahogany, I drove myself home and she was up making her late night cup of tea. One look at me and she reached into the kitchen draw where we kept one of our many guns around the house. Justine would take on the world behind her only son. I quickly talked her down and gave her the quick version of what had gone down. She complimented the patchwork that Mahogany's girl had done and warned me not to take another bullet for a woman I wasn't claiming. I only nodded, thinking in my head that I was more than intrigued with Mahogany Wright.

So much so that I decided to take a backseat to finding out who was at her head. It would've been easy for me to do my own recon, but I learned that Mahogany wasn't a woman who needed saving. She wanted to do things on her own terms, in her own time. I respected that, but it only made me want to cover her more.

"I don't know what it is, ma," I finally let out. "You know me. I'm very selective when it comes to my time. I don't allow women in my space longer than two days and I damn sure ain't taking no bullets for 'em. Mahogany though..."

"You think you met your match?" She smirked.

"Jury's still out on that. She definitely has my attention."

"Hmph, anyone that I catch a bullet for would have mine too."

"Yeah, back to this, though," I said, redirecting her back to the desk and the photos.

"This is pretty simple to me, son. Get the witnesses to recant and dead them. I will say this, no matter how you slice it, can't nobody convince me that Curtis "Coolie" Wright killed two niggas and got caught. That nigga and Dough got more bodies buried than your lifespan. It's clear that he was set up. Now, *the who* is the mystery. I can only tell you that it's surely someone he knows."

"I concluded the same."

"I'm actually surprised that he's just getting around to taking care of it."

"Me too. He all but said that it required a Blackstone touch to get the results he's looking for."

"Well," she grabbed my hand, "make your dad proud and give the man what he paid for." She kissed the back of my hand and went to leave the office.

"So much for retirement," I let out, sarcastically.

She stopped short and held the door open. "You're only dipping your toe back in. In and out like a robbery."

"Like I was never there." She tilted her head, and I did the same as she closed the door behind her. *There's no better time than the present,"* I said out loud to myself, deciding that I would make my move tonight.

"I hope this nigga ain't on bullshit. I really need this money."

"You crazy as hell. This nigga basically had us snatched up off the street and you think he really bout to give us some money? I don't want no parts of this shit. Never wanted no parts of this shit to begin with."

"You're dragging it, Mel. Didn't nobody snatch us off the street. We willingly got in the car."

"Are you fucking dumb?! It's late as hell and a blacked-out truck came through the hood and big, black, burly looking nigga told us to get in. You think I was gonna tell him no? These scary niggas didn't even protest."

"Will y'all both shut the fuck up?! A nigga tryna think."

*"No, Wes, **you** shut the fuck up. You tryna think is what got us in this situation in the first place. You and them co—."*

"Shut yo ass up!"

I watched the group go at it from behind the two-way mirror, inside of the industrial sized warehouse I owned in Coney Island. The scene before me was comical and it seemed that only one person in the group had the mind to question the motives of a man they had yet to see. The most they knew was they were being offered $10,000 each to right a wrong. At least that was all that was detailed in the text message along with the time to meet.

I had one of my people pick the foursome up and drop them off to me. After going over Coolie's case in detail and the mountain of evidence his defense team had presented to the court, along with his airtight alibi, I was more than compelled to handle this shit on his behalf. It was crazy how the boys played dirty when they couldn't touch you. Coolie was a kingpin. One who stayed under the radar and out the way. There was no doubt in my mind that the person who had put this whole play together was someone he knew. Likely a fucking hater and a snake.

The group before me had been used as pawns in this whole game. At the end of the day this shit was chess not checkers. With Coolie being the man my father had spoken highly of in the past, I knew that he'd used this time to move the pieces on the board. All he needed was to be free to expose and dead the nigga once the opportunity presented itself. For now, I would do my part.

Refocusing back on the scene before me, the group had turned it up a notch and were in a full-blown argument. Unbeknownst to them, I hit the record button for the hidden camera I had set up after they'd mentioned the offer of money and the black truck they'd been picked up in.

*"No, you shut up! This shit is **all** your fault. Those were **your** guns in that car."* The prettier of the two females stood with her hand pointed in one of the dude's faces. *"Then you,"* she pointed to the other, *"driving around like you on Grand Theft Auto. We got pulled over cause of y'all!"*

"So, we made y'all sign those papers too, right? We in the same fucking boat, Mel. Beefing with me ain't gon' change what happened or get that nigga outta jail. It was either him or us, and we," he gestured with his hands to signal the group, *"made a decision. We needed a get outta jail free card and we got it."*

"He's right, Mel," the not so cute friend cosigned.

"Y'all are really sick in the head. We put a man behind bars for some shit we didn't even see happen. We were nowhere near the crime scene, and we don't even know the people who got killed."

"Yeah, well, if it's bothering you so bad, take yo ass up to the courthouse and take the charge for them two guns," Wes spat.

"Fuck you!" The girl shook her head and sat back down with her arms folded across her chest. *"I hope you sleep well at night."*

"Yep. Like a fucking baby."

I decided that I was gonna kill the Wes dude first. I had to. Ending the recording, I opened the door and made myself known.

"I'll make this quick. Who I am is not important but in front of you is a pen and paper. On that paper I need you to detail the night of April 10th, 2022, as you recall it. The next sheet of paper you'll address to ADA Thomason. It'll be a letter recanting your statements given to the police on the night in question regarding a murder you all **did not** see committed. You'll express your deepest apologies to the Wright family for the pain they endured due to your lack of integrity. Once that's done, you'll get your money and be on your way."

"And how do we know you're serious?" The more facially challenged of the women questioned.

"Check under y'all seats." Watching them look, I shook my head, completely disgusted with the two dudes. They were so blinded by the offer of money, neither of their minds had yet to compute that they were in a fucked-up predicament.

"Oooh, wee," the Wes dude cheered, thumbing through the counterfeit bills in his envelope. His comrade was just as excited, along with the female seated next to Mel.

"What's the ADA name again?" The other dude asked out loud.

"Thomason," Wes answered.

"Cool."

They got to writing while Mel was hesitant for a few seconds. I nodded in her direction, and she put pen to paper. For fifteen minutes, they wrote in silence and once done, all papers were passed down to me. As I gathered the papers, there was a knock at the door.

"Come in," I called out.

The door opened, and Mahogany walked in. At first glance, I noticed the hard look on her face. There was no trace of a smile, and her body language was anything but friendly. Even still, she was bad as fuck. With each step she took, her heels echoed throughout the room. Stopping next to me, she eyed everyone at the table. Her eyes lingered on Mel's longer than the others.

"Melanie, right?" She inquired. The sound of silence was almost deafening. With fear of confirming verbally, Melanie nodded her head. Mahogany then pointed to the other three that occupied the other seats and called them out by name. "Jackie, Quan, and Wesley."

"Nah, I don't know a Wesley," Wes spoke up. "If we're all done here, I'ma head out. Thanks for this," he held up the envelope. "And I hope that letter gets dude home. I hope he understands that we had to do what we had to do. Come on, bro." He tapped his boy's chair, who stood at his request. "Y'all coming?" He asked the girls once he was near the door to exit.

Pfft, pfft. Two shots from my FNX 45 dropped Quan and Wes, causing high pitch screams from the girls. The silencer that had been screwed onto the gun made it so that no one knew what was happening until their bodies hit the ground. Mahogany turned and silenced both Justine and Melanie with two shots to the head.

"We need to talk," Mahogany stated, securing her gun back in her oversized purse.

"Before or after I clean this up?" I asked, looking around at the bodies.

"I'm sure you have people for that, Mr. Blackstone." The way my name slid off her tongue made my dick jump. "I did my research. I'll be out front." Turning on her heels, she casually stepped over Wes' and Quan's bodies and left the room.

Oh, yeah, that's Coolie's daughter for sure. Ain't no denying that, I said to myself as I pulled out my phone to call my clean up guy.

Chapter Eleven

MAHOGANY

I LOOKED AT THE TEXT MESSAGE FROM BRISCOE AND immediately became irritated. I'd stayed with Tiff a little longer to keep her company until Money came back from the store.

"Look at this bullshit," I said to her while holding my phone up for her to see. "*Now* he wanna reach out after two fucking days of being M.I.A. I swear this nigga gon' make me go upside his shit."

Tiff just shook her head and picked up her own phone. "Go head and answer."

"I am, but I'm not gonna text back. I'ma call his ass. I need to hear the lie when I ask him what the fuck is up." Tapping his contact, I hit the call button, and the phone rang once before I was sent to voicemail. "I know damn well," I said out loud while pressing call again only to get the same result. Going back to the text thread, I responded.

He texted back immediately, pissin' me off.

> Beautii Dad: I'm handling something right now, Mahogany, damn. Are you home?

> Me: Nah, nigga. I'm in my skin, fuck outta here!

I dropped the phone in my purse just as my mother walked back in the room with Beautii. Tiff gave me a knowing look but didn't say anything. Briscoe not wanting to talk on the phone but wanting to know my whereabouts was crazy. And after the last 48 hours I just had, didn't no motherfucka need to have tabs on me unless I volunteered the information.

"Is it safe for me to be in here now?" Beautii questioned with her hands up.

Tiff smiled. "You good, Beautii girl," she assured her.

My phone rang in my bag and thinking it was Briscoe, I was ready to decline the call, but it was Monk Man. Seeing his burner phone number on my caller id, my eyebrow raised, and I answered the call.

"You straight?" I asked as the call connected.

"You busy right now?"

"Nah, wassup?"

"Man, you ain't gon' believe what I just found out about one of your people."

"Well, make me a believer." He went to speak and gave me an earful of some shit I definitely wasn't expecting. **"When you found this out?"**

"About an hour ago. I had to cross check a couple things before bringing the news to you. I connected the dots and I'm sorry to tell you that this is what it is."

"I'm not. Send me what you have to my business email. Thanks, Monk Man."

"No problem." He hung up and I went to tell Tiff about the phone call when Money walked in.

"Here you go, Beautii." He handed her a black plastic bag and she reached for it with excitement. "I got you some broccoli and cheddar soup, mama," he said to Tiff.

"Thank you, Montez. You gotta go, Mahogany?" She asked me, clearly picking up on my body language.

"Umm, yeah. Remember, one more day and you outta here."

"One more day," she repeated. "Come gimmie a hug, Beautii girl." While she said her goodbyes to my mother and Beautii, I left the room to call Mo.

What were the odds of me calling and her telling me she was following Pete. I told her the news Monk Man had dropped on me and she was just as shocked. To add insult to injury, she'd followed him to what sounded like the same hotel Santana was staying in. The wheels in my head got to turning and I told her to stand down. She had a more imperative matter to handle which was the Derek situation. I had something for Pete's ass. Before we ended the call, I had her drop her location and sure enough, Pete was at the same Hilton hotel I visited two days ago.

Ending the call, I pulled Money to the side.

"Ay, I need you to go check on the traps for me today. I know you wanna stay here with Tiff, but she's a big girl and she will be fine. Mo is out tying up the loose end for the situation regarding Monk Man, so I need you on this, okay."

"Aight. I'll make it happen."

"Thank you. Oh, and don't worry about tappin' in with Pete. I'ma have a one on one with him."

"Aight." We both walked back over to Tiff, and I gave her a half hug.

"I need you to take your time and heal. I know it's better said than done, but I can't have you out here not moving at your best, Tiff."

"Yeah, I hear you. I'ma do what I can but don't count on me being down for long. You know I gotta get my lick back and then some."

"I'm already knowing. And you know we riding soon as the time is right. For now, let me handle what's within my reach."

Leaving the hospital, I got a call from my mechanic. This would be the first time I heard from him since my car had been dropped off. I wasn't worried about the car being fixed. Manny had been my mechanic for years and he knew me and my family well.

"Wassup, Manny? What's the damage?"

"Hey, Mahogany. The damage wasn't too bad. We can have it delivered to you tomorrow at the club."

"That works for me. You could've texted that, though."

"I know. I called so you can see this." The phone signaled an incoming facetime call from him. I hit the video icon and Manny appeared with what looked like a small battery pack held up to the camera. "Do you know what this is?"

"I hope not what I think it is."

"Unfortunately, yes. I found it under your car. I wanted to bring it to your attention before I got rid of it."

I went silent, replaying the highway incident in my head and how everything had occurred. From the way the driver pulled up alongside of me to that anxious feeling I got. I was being set up.

"Thanks, Manny. I really appreciate this call. Don't get rid of it. Any way you can dismantle the device without breaking it? I wanna have my guy look into it."

"Sure. I can do that."

"Cool. Do that and put it in my glove compartment, please."

"No problem. We'll drop off tomorrow, you just hit me with a time that's convenient for you."

"Will do."

"What was that about?" My mother asked, closing the door behind Beautii and getting in on the passenger side.

"Manny found a tracking device on my car."

"Get the hell outta here. When?"

"I guess just now." Hopping in the car, I started it up and pulled off.

"Who the hell would..." she paused and turned to Beautii. "Put your headphones on, Beautii." Beautii complied and put her face in her phone. "Who the hell would put a tracking device on your car?"

"Shit, clearly someone who wants to track my movements. Likely the same person or persons that almost had us run off the road."

"Yeah, we gotta nip this shit in the bud and quick. I'm doing my best to let you handle your shit but I'm feeling like I need to step in and shake some shit up."

I nodded. "Not necessary, ma. I got it handled."

"Well, it would probably prove beneficial to you if you had your brother by your side. And before you shut the idea down, give it some thought. Yeah, you have Mo and Tiff, but another set of eyes couldn't hurt, especially with what's been going on."

"I hear you." Steering the wheel with one hand, I used the other to text Scooter.

I sent the address to the Hilton hotel to Scooter with a simple instruction for him to follow Pete. I didn't care if he took him on a journey, he'd better put his car on cruise control to ride it out. Pete had a blind date with death tonight and I would be the one making the introduction.

♫*NIGGAS, BETTER GRAB A SEAT, GRAB ON YOUR DICK AS THIS bitch gets deep. Deeper than the pussy of a bitch six feet. Stiff dicks feel sweet in this little petite, young bitch from the street guaranteed to stay down, used to bring work outta town on Greyhound. ♫*

Lil Kim's verse on Biggie's "Get Money" played throughout the club as I made my rounds, checking the temperature of the crowd. I'd reopened my doors last night for the first time since the shooting, and the people were lined up down the block, waiting to get in. As they filed in, I saw dollar signs. Any money that we missed while closed was sure to be doubled. Scanning the crowd, I saw Pete walk through the door with his driver and as if he knew where I'd be, he turned his head in my direction and caught my eye. Navigating the crowd, I walked over to the bar.

"Hey, Corbin," I called out to the bartender who was manning the bar solo and doing a damn good job.

"I'll be right there," she yelled out and came over after taking care of a customer. "Hey, you need anything?"

"Yeah. Let me get a bottle of water and send Cherokee to my office in ten minutes."

"Got you." She turned to grab my water, and a customer called out to her. Turning back to me, she gave me the bottle and I nodded in the direction of the guy who stood at the end of the bar with his money in the air.

"Handle your business and don't forget to send Cherokee my way in ten minutes."

"Okay." I started to walk in the direction that Pete and his driver stood near the exit. I made sure to take slow strides, wanting Pete to know he was on my time.

"Follow me to my office," I instructed, and he fell in step behind me.

"You know you're sitting on a goldmine with this place, right," Pete let out as we entered my office.

"I do," I replied and gestured for him to have a seat.

"I've been sitting all day, I'd rather stand, thanks." He was in defense mode. That was one sign of guilt.

"Fine by me," I acknowledged with a shrug of my shoulders. "You want a drink?"

He smirked. "Come on now, Mahogany, let's not play these games. First, you have Morae pop up unannounced and now you got your people following me. I've been in this game long enough to know the signs. So wassup? Real nigga to real nigga, what you on my head about?"

Taking the cap off my water, I took a swig. I watched for any sudden movements from his driver while still maintaining a clear focus on Pete. "Real nigga to real nigga, huh?"

"Yeah. My money ain't right or something? Somebody on my team fucking up? What?"

"Remember the night I called a meeting and told everyone in attendance about the shooting that happened here?"

"I ain't have shit to do with that. And I know that's not why you had me followed today."

"True. Back to what I was saying, though. That night, I asked you if you'd heard any noise surrounding that personal matter I had to handle around your way. Your words were, and I'm paraphrasing, 'if you heard any noise, it would've been silenced before it came to my doorstep. You know, with you being all about family.' Correct me if I'm wrong."

"More less."

"Cool." My phone chimed. Pulling it from my pants pocket, I noticed two text messages. One from Santana and the other from Justice. Putting Justice's text on hold, I opened Santana's.

Opp: I'm outside.

Me: Come in and let the bouncer know that you're meeting with me. They'll bring you back here to my office.

"Mahogany, I'm a man of little patience," Pete stated, "and out of respect for you, I came to you directly to see what was up. I'm starting to regret that." I went to respond to him and was interrupted by a knock at the door. Figuring it was Cherokee, I called out for her to open it.

"Hey, boss lady. You wanted to see me?" Cherokee entered my office, fresh off the stage, giving every bit of video vixen. Pasties covered her nipples and the thong she had on seemed to lose its way between her big, round, peached shaped ass. Under the light, her skin glistened and sparkled from the body glitter mixed with sweat.

"Yes. Can you take this gentleman," I pointed to Pete's driver, Drew, "and give him the VIP treatment? The works."

Cherokee licked her lips and flicked her tongue ring in and out of her mouth. "I'd be happy to." She eyed Drew when she spoke. Drew looked to Pete who gave a silent blessing with a nod of his head. "I ain't gon' bite you, boo. I promise." She flirted, taking his hand in hers and escorting him out of the office. The confidence in her stride easily captivated any man. The body that came with it made it that much easier. Once they were out of the office, I refocused on Pete.

"Pete, when I first took my seat as head of The Table, I looked each of you in the eye and told you what it was that I expected and what I was going to give in return."

"Ma—."

"Yasir Janard Yusef, how do you know him?" I cut him off. His left eye twitched, but the rest of his face remained neutral. My father had always taught me to be cognizant of one's body language. It only took one slight move to detect dishonesty. So far, I'd detected two separate gestures from Pete. Coupled with his defensive stance and what Monk Man had told me, I was only giving him the opportunity to be honest for fucks sake.

"The name sounds familiar. One that I've heard before, but then again, I come in contact with a lot of people in this business so it's not uncommon for a name to escape me."

Hearing a knock at my office door, I walked over to answer it. Without asking who it was, I opened the door and stepped back to allow Santana entry.

"Them niggas you got up there bouncing shit sho is uptight than a motherfucka," Santana said as he walked in. "Oh, my bad. I didn't know you were in a meeting. I can go over to the bar and come back when you're done."

Pete didn't bother turning around when he heard Santana's voice, so I offered him a seat.

"You sure you don't wanna sit down, Pete?" I asked.

"Nah, I'm good. I actually need to get going. I got shit to do," he replied.

"Oh, leaving so soon?" I asked, sarcastically. "We were just about to figure some shit out. It won't be too much longer. Santana, this is Pete. Pete, this is Santana." I made the introduction and stood back to watch their interaction.

Pete held his hand out for Santana to shake while Santana gave him a head nod. *Smart move,* I said to myself, giving Santana silent props for his response.

"Since when do we talk business in front of random niggas? For all that, Drew could've stayed. You already know him."

"So, y'all don't know each other?" I pointed back and forth between him and Santana.

"Ain't never seen this man a day in my life," Pete expressed with a straight face.

I nodded and walked around my desk. Reaching under it, I pulled my Glock 9 out of the compartment I had my designer add on for me in case of emergencies. At any given time, anywhere I stood in my office, a gun was accessible to me. A bitch stayed strapped like a dyke with her piece. Holding the gun in front of me, I had a vice grip on the heavy metal.

"Damn, that's what it's come to?" Pete questioned solemnly, but I didn't miss the scowl he threw in Santana's direction.

"Here's the thing, Pete, whenever I ask someone a question, more often than not, I already know the answer. So, what I do is, give you the benefit of doubt. And you at your big ass age gon' sit here and try to insult my intelligence and blatantly lie about something as simple as knowing a nigga." I upped the Glock and aimed it at his chest. "If you'll lie to me, you'll steal from me, Pete. And if you'll steal from me, I'm almost certain you'll try to kill me."

"Lie? Mahogany, I'm a grown ass—."

Pop! I sent a shot in his direction that landed right between his eyes, and he dropped to the floor with a loud thud. "Shut yo lyin' ass up," I spat. I then turned the gun on Santana.

"You know this the second time you done pulled a gun out on me, sis."

"I promise this will be the last time, cause if you don't come up with a logical explanation as to why this lyin' bastard was at your hotel earlier, I'm gonna have to go back to being the only child people know of."

"Maann, it ain't even what you think it is."

"It ain't? Cause what I'm thinking is that you just as much of a snake as this dead nigga here." I nodded towards Pete's dead body.

"I know what it looks like but it ain't. I've known Snake, well Pete as you know him, for years. His people have history with my pops. Long story short, I had reached out to him when I touched down just to chop it up and see how he was doing and shit. Come to find out he's a part of your shit. I ask about getting put on and he all but told me that he didn't have that pull but he was working on something on the inside that was sure to put him in position. Seeing as nobody knows about my family outside of my pops, he didn't have any problem telling me what that plan was."

With a dead look on my face and my gun pointed at his chest, I waited for him to continue. "And?"

"Shit, it should be self-explanatory. That nigga was not a fan of yours and was plotting to get you outta here. I guess it's safe to say that you still can't go around killin' nigga's family members and leave them alive to sort out the memories." He was fishing, but a bitch was born at night not last night. "I can see it in your eyes that you don't believe me. Well, come outside with me for a minute, I wanna show you something."

With a raised brow, I lowered my gun to my side. "Outside?"

"Yeah. I got something to show you."

"Uh huh." I picked my phone up from the desk and dialed Scooter. "What kinda car you driving and where you park at?"

"A navy-blue Toyota Corolla. It's parked on the side of the club."

"Scooter, have Bear go out and check for a navy-blue Toyota Corolla on the side of the club," I instructed. **"Also, send the cleaners up to the VIP room Cherokee is in. She had a long night and I'm sure she showed out with this one. And then, send them to my office, I had to straighten some shit out myself. Thank you."** Ending the call, I gestured towards the door. "Let's go."

Outside, I followed Santana over to his car with every intention of cutting his lifespan short if he was playing with me. Hearing about his history with Pete and finding out that Pete had been plotting made me uneasy. Crazy how the nigga had the nickname *Snake* and that's exactly what he turned out to be. It was still fuck his rat ass godson and his dead ass for that matter. Once I made a decision and followed through there was no need in feeling sorry about shit. It was what the fuck it was so long as I deemed it so.

Santana walked around the back of the car and stopped at the trunk. "You straight?"

"Nigga, get to what you got me out here for." Shaking his head, he popped the trunk and inside was a man shivering with duct tape wrapped around his head, preventing him from seeing. Upon further inspection, I could see that his hands and feet were bound as well. "Who the hell is this and why the hell would you pull up to my club with this nigga in your trunk?"

Santana looked at me then back down at the man. "This the nigga who tried to run you off the road. He's also the father of the lil' nigga you bodied." My lips formed a straight line because again, he was fishing. And I didn't know what Yasir's dad looked like to confirm. "Let me make it make sense to you. Pete let him know that it was you who killed his son. Pete assured him that he was gonna take care of it after he," he pointed to the man, "vowed to get his own revenge. Now, according to the dead, he was already plotting on you and his god son, son of man in the truck being killed only added fuel to the fire. Long story short, he had a tracker put on your car, hence how he knew you'd be on the highway."

"Or yo ass told him and that's how he knew." I side eyed him.

"What you'll soon learn about me is, I'm all about my paper. And while I came back to the East Coast to fix my relationship with the family, I still gotta get to that bag. Me tryna set you up don't benefit me, sis. Coolie left you in position. This shit don't move without yo say so. All a nigga tryna do is be in the family business. If I gotta end a couple niggas to prove my loyalty, then point me in that direction."

"Start with this one and make it clean. Hit the number I texted you from when it's done." My phone buzzed in my pocket, and it was another message from Justice. Reading the message, my heart rate quickened. Pivoting, I walked briskly back to the club, leaving Santana to tie up his loose end. Him getting the deed done didn't make him loyal in my eyes but it was a step in the right direction.

FROM MY CAR, I WATCHED JUSTICE WALK OUT OF THE warehouse he'd called me to and shook my head. I had been so wrapped up in all that I had going on, he'd managed to get one up on me in the most unsuspecting way. I had questions and needed him to answer the who, when, why, and how's. How did he locate the remaining witnesses on my dad's case? When did he find out about them? Who was his contact and had he known who I was before our initial interaction at his carwash?

As I'd mentioned to him, I had done my research and the shit I'd uncovered about the Blackstone's in the underworld was heavy. You see, when Justice left my club the night he was shot and insisted that I look him up, I knew the information I wanted couldn't be found in your normal background check site that you found on Google. The way he carried himself let me know that he was somebody. Monk Man did his due diligence, and I concluded that Mr. Blackstone came from a powerful lineage in the underworld. His father was a certified hitta and seeing the way Justice had taken care of business, there was no doubt in my mind that he was, too.

"You gonna let me in or you gonna leave me standing out here?" He asked from where he now stood at my window, with his hand on the door handle.

I hit the locks to allow him entry. The same gun I'd used to kill the two women inside sat on my lap and my finger rested comfortably on the trigger. Opening the door, he got in. Before he could close the door, a black Sprinter van slowly crept up on the block and drove around to the back of the warehouse. I took note of his calmness and noticed how it settled my body.

"Your crew?" I questioned.

"Yeah." It was late and with the warehouse being on the dead-end street, no one would think to drive this way if it wasn't someone he knew.

"Tell me, Justice, did someone hire you to take me out?"

He stared in my eyes and licked his full lips. "Tell me, Mahogany, what would a woman as beautiful as yourself have done to deserve such fate?"

"You'd be surprised at the monster some may peg me out to be. But please, don't answer my question with a question." I cocked the gun back and pointed it at his forehead. "Did someone hire you to kill me?"

"No." He didn't flinch nor blink.

"Why'd you call me here tonight?"

"Cause I know if I was in your position, I would want someone to extend the same courtesy to me if the opportunity presented itself."

"And what position is that?"

"You're the daughter of a kingpin who was framed for two murders he didn't commit, who's currently fighting time, sitting in a place he shouldn't be. And anything you can do to aid in that process, you've done and you're still willing to do. That's something I can respect. So, while your father may see it differently, I couldn't see myself completing the deed without you getting your just due."

"Did you know who my father was before or after we met?"

"Your father is a friend of the family. He and my dad had history. He told me about you before we actually met."

Putting my gun down, I thought back to when I mentioned Justice' name to my father during a visit. He asked his last name, but at the time, I didn't know it. The world was too small.

"So, what now? Dead witnesses are cool and all, but I doubt if that'll be enough to get him home," I let out.

"He'll be home. People pay me for results. Coolie knew what he was doing when he hired me. You don't worry about that. How are things on your end?"

"Why? You gon' come and fixed my problems, too?" I asked, leaning over the armrest.

He did the same, leaving our faces only a few inches from each other. "I could. All you gotta do is say the word. Besides, somebody out there still gotta see me behind that shooting."

"That's already taken care of, along with everything else," I assured him, even though there were still some loose ends I needed to tie up.

"See, now you keeping me in the dark."

"Nah. It's just my business is my business."

"Tell me a secret," he said, leaning in closer.

"What?" I retorted, thrown off by his statement and him leaning closer. I took in his facial features and found myself wanting to rub my hand across his blemish free skin just to see if it was as soft as it appeared to be.

"Tell me a secret. Something that only you know and may be afraid to share."

"You know we just killed four people and there's bodies in that warehouse, right?" I said in my attempt to avoid the question.

"That's been taken care of. My people are very efficient, and they know when I call that I expect things done in a timely manner. Your secret?"

I smized. "The seat of my thong is covered in my juices, right now."

"I said tell me a secret, Mahogany. Something that I don't already know." The way the words dripped from his lips, my nipples hardened. This nigga had it! And if I didn't get him out of my car right now, he was sure to have me.

My phone rang and I smirked at him before answering the call on speaker.

"Maintenance is done," Scooter reported.

"Cherokee handled VIP?"

"Like a pro."

I nodded and smiled. **"That's what I like to hear. I'll be there to lock up."**

"Aight. I'll wait on you."

I ended the call and turned back to Justice. "I gotta get going. Do me a favor, when you meet up with my father again, don't tell him about me being here."

"I got you."

"And thank you."

"For?"

"Taking care of this situation. My father doesn't make decisions without fully thinking his plans through from start to finish. If he reached out to you it was for good reason."

"No sweat. Text me when you make it back to the club." He put his hand on the door handle, and I pulled him back. "Wassup?"

Void of words, I planted a single kiss on his lips and pulled back. "Get home safe, Mr. Blackstone."

"You too, gangsta."

He proceeded to get out of the car, and I drove off into the night feeling like I'd just met my match.

Chapter Twelve

TIFFANY

"Ooh, ooh, shit," I moaned in my sleep, stuck in a full-blown wet dream starring Money. He'd licked me from the crack of my ass to the top of my pussy and had me screaming out his name.

No man had ever taken the time to explore my body in such a way. It was clear that he was skilled in the art of pussy eating. Shit, he was the pussy monster. The pussy eating champ! Feeling my orgasm mounting, I reached down and pulled the hood of my clit between my thumb and pointer finger to massage it. My heartbeat raced, and I knew I was close, so fuckin' close.

"That's right, mama. Give that shit up. Make it rain in my mouth." My eyes popped open upon hearing Money's voice.

"Montezzz." I dragged his name the same way he dragged his tongue down my slit.

I should've known that it wasn't a dream. The feeling was too intense to not be true. He looked up from between my legs, flashed a sexy smile, and went back to feasting on my kitty.

"Cum for me, Tiff. Let that shit go, mama. I promise daddy gon' give you more." With his encouragement, he flicked his tongue over my clit while simultaneously brushing it against my fingers. My body withered as I tried to scoot back on the bed, only for him to grab hold of my ass to keep me in place.

"Shiiittt, you gon' make me cum, Montez," I cried out. In my attempt to wiggle out of the grip he had on my waist, I shifted too quick, causing a pain to shoot through my chest where I'd been shot. "Ouuchhh!" I yelled out, pushing his head from between my legs. The feeling of bliss had turned into pain real quick.

"What, what happen?" He questioned, as he popped up with a bare chest, a worried look on his face, and his mouth wet from my essence.

"My chest," I groaned out in pain with my hand on the dressing.

"Damn, bae. I'm sorry, mama. Here, let me get you the pain medication." He got up and I waved him off.

"No, I'm okay. It will subside. No more pills." Closing my eyes, I rocked back and forth in an attempt to block out the pain.

"Well, all that rocking and shit ain't gon' make it better. Come 'ere." He slid in the bed next to me and had me sit up so that my back was facing him.

"Where are your clothes, Montez?" I asked, realizing that he only had on his boxers and Nike socks.

"I took them off last night. Well, late this morning when I got here. I know how you are about clothes in your bed." He gently massaged my neck and worked his way down to my shoulders.

I was on day seven of the suggested bed rest from my doctor and mandatory break from my father. Money had become a permanent fixture around my house the entire time. While he was gone for most of the day, he rested his head in my bed the last six nights, even though I'd offered him one of my two guest bedrooms. I agreed that he could sleep in bed with me under the condition that he slept with his basketball shorts on. He'd adhered to that up until now.

It was hard enough watching him walk around in a towel after he showered. And now he'd given my pussy a good tongue lashing that had me squeezing my legs closed to stop my clit from thumpin'. I'd done a good job at keeping him at bay after we'd hunched in Mo's bathroom, but this nigga was making it hard to hold it down. And I knew he was doing it on purpose, too.

"I thought we agreed that we weren't going there right now," I said, reminding him of our talk in the hospital before I was discharged. I turned my body to face him. "I'm still healing."

"Girl, I agreed that I wasn't gonna fuck on you. I ain't say nothin' bout lickin' on that wet box. That pussy phat as hell, too. When I got you in the bathroom, I didn't get a good look, but ooouu wee. She was sitting up waiting for me this morning." He nodded at my exposed mound, making me snatch up the sheet to cover myself.

"I get off house arrest today," I changed the subject. Knowing him and his dirty mind, he could talk about my pussy all day.

"I know. How you feeling?" He laid back on the bed with his hand behind his head and the other rested in his boxers. I caught him licking his lips then curling the top one up to smell it. The man was a lunatic.

"I feel like I've been left out of the loop. Kinda like I'm behind." During bedrest, Mahogany kept me up to speed on the day to day and had Scooter temporarily hold my spot as her security until I was back. Although I didn't like it, I appreciated that both she and Mo made sure that I didn't miss a beat. It was nothing like being in the thick of things, though.

Mahogany assured me that expansion would be put on hold until I returned. Today was that day and I couldn't wait to pull up to the meeting later on.

"Well, you already know we haven't found the nigga behind your shooting. Business has been business and any other shit you may need to know is female shit that I'm sure they've caught you up on. Shit been quiet for the most part, but you know I'm still lying in wait for the shooter to slip up in some shape or form."

"I'm starting to think whoever it was may have been someone Pete knew. I'm still pissed that I missed the red flags with his ass."

It was my job to watch out for snakes in the grass and I'd missed that one. When Mahogany told me she had to cut Pete's lights off, I was surprised. Even more surprised when she revealed that her brother had a part to play in Pete being exposed. I only hoped that it was the end of niggas coming at our heads. Only I couldn't say for sure until the person behind my shooting was six feet under hell.

"Shit, who knows. Niggas be so flawed these days, you don't know who to trust. To keep it all the way funky witchu, I been keeping an eye on that nigga Briscoe for a minute. And I still got my eyes open for this Santana dude, too."

"That's why we trust no one," I declared.

"You don't trust me?" He asked, tugging on the sheet, making it slip from my hand. "Look at her," he marveled.

I used my hand to cover my pussy and shook my head. "To answer your question, no, I don't trust you. At the same time, I don't believe you'll ever do anything to intentionally cause me harm."

Scooting forward on the bed, he grabbed me by my legs and pulled me forward. Making it so that my legs were rested on top of his, he rubbed my thighs.

"I respect that, mama. Check this out though, I know you're happy to get back in the field and all, but I really need you to chill." I went to object to the bullshit he was saying, and he squeezed my thigh. "Wait, hear me out. I'm not saying not to handle yo shit. I'm just saying be mindful that you have an injury. Don't be out here moving crazy. No matter what you've convinced yourself of in your mind, you're still healing."

He was right. I was still in recovery, but I wasn't going to move as if I was. That would be a sure sign of weakness.

"Okay, I hear you. I'll take it easy but I'm not about to be moving around like I'm handicap, either."

"Didn't expect you to."

"Yeah, well, I'm just letting you know."

"I'm gonna miss coming home to you. Laying up witchu, watching all that *CSI* shit."

I laughed. "Shut up. That show is informative, don't even cap."

"Yeah, that shit straight. I actually stayed up and watched a few more episodes the other night when you fell asleep on the couch. You look so peaceful when you sleep, knowing you're a hell raiser when you get up." He chuckled and I gave him the finger.

"See, don't say I never put you on to nothing. Now, you can go and share your new show with yo hoes." I stuck my tongue out at him.

His face turned up in a frown. "What kind of lame ass nigga you take me for? Why would I share our shit with the next bitch?"

I giggled a little. "Fix your face. You know what I mean."

"Nah, I don't, Tiff."

"So, you don't have bitches now, Montez? Come on, be forreal."

"I never said I didn't. What I *am* saying is don't insult me by thinking what I do with you, I do with other bitches. And if you just fuck with a nigga forreal, I could leave all that shit alone and be a one-woman man."

"You don't think you should wanna be that even if it wasn't for me?" I cocked my head to the side.

"You know there's piss in the dating pool, right? Ain't none of these bitches worth the investment of my time, my good heart, and this A1 smoke pole." He grinned and winked at me.

"Smoke what... nevermind. That's my cue." Throwing my leg over his, I went to stand, only to be pulled back down, landing on his hard on.

"Lemme buss yo pretty ass up real quick. Put this dick in yo spine and show you why you bout to be calling me daddy soon." He licked my neck, and I shivered.

"No, Montez," I said in a less than convincing tone.

"Girl, come on. You better get this dick. You'll have an extra pep in yo step for your first day back. Sit up for a second." I did as he said, not bothering to protest. He pulled off his boxers and I bit my lip. Leaning back on the bed, he patted his thigh. "Come on and climb up here, mama."

My heart beat my mind again, and I found myself climbing on top of him. He slapped my ass as I slid down on his dick slowly.

"Ahhhh, yess," I moaned out loud in great satisfaction as his dick pushed into me to the hilt. I basked in every stroke and threw my head back, with my mouth agape. It was *too* good, too damn good.

Money sat up, grabbed me by waist, and rocked me back and forth, letting his dick hit my walls, making my body shake as I came.

"Uh huh, wet that dick up, Tiff. Ooouu shit. Quit playin' wit a nigga. This dick yours, you hear me?" He kissed around my bandage and up to my neck before stopping at my lips.

Soft, loving kisses were placed on my lips and I found myself tearing up. I don't know if it was the dick or the love I felt through his kisses. It may have been a mixture of both. Whatever it was, the moment was *perfect.* So perfect, that it forced me to speak the thoughts I'd kept hidden for years.

"I love you, Montez."

"I know, baby. Daddy love you too, so much. So fuckin' much. Goddamn, I'm bout to nut. You ready to be a mommy?"

I didn't respond. Instead, I spun around and did Trina proud by keeping the dick inside. Planting my feet flat on the bed, I looked back at him with a wink. He gave my ass another smack.

"You play with my heart, I'ma fuck you up."

With a smirk on his face, he put both hands behind his head. "Playin' witcho heart would be like playin' with my own. Go head and show out on that dick, mama." We just sealed the deal. Montez was mine and I was his.

As I got dressed for the meeting at The Table, I found myself thinking about my decision to take a chance on Money. I wasn't second guessing my decision, I just hoped that he understood all that came with me. His mention of me being a mommy for the second time put me on edge. Money knew my situation, so I couldn't understand why he kept mentioning this baby. The last thing I wanted was for him to set an expectation of me that he knew I couldn't deliver on.

"Bae, your phone ringing," he called out from my bedroom.

"Can you bring it to me, please?" Carefully pulling the bodysuit over my head, I snapped it and shimmied my way into a pair of jeans.

"Ass phat as fuck," Money complimented and squeezed my booty.

I smiled. "Who's calling?"

"Yo dad." Kissing my cheek, he left the bathroom.

"Hey, dad," I answered the call on speaker.

"Hey, boo, it's mommy."

"Oh, hey ma. Why you callin' from dad's phone?"

"Cause this my man."

I laughed at her response. **"You right, you right. Wassup, what y'all doing?"**

"Nothing much, watching a movie. I wanted to check on you and see how you were doing."

"I'm good, mommy. Getting ready to head out soon to meet up with the girls."

"Don't go out there doing the most, Tiffany. You're not 100% yet. Take it easy."

"Oh, God. You sound like Money. I know I'm not 100%. I got this."

"Yeah, that's why I like him. But you heard what yo momma said."

"Yep."

"Alright, I love you. Here go your father."

"Back at it, huh?" My dad asked.

"Yep. You wanna lecture me about taking it easy, too?"

"No, you're my daughter. I know you know what to do. So long as you tell me you're ready to be back, then you're ready to be back."

Knowing he needed to hear me say the words, I did. **"Yes, dad, I'm ready to be back."**

"That's what it is, then. I took care of that situation for you, too."

"What situation might that be?"

"Your shooter no longer walks among us."

"Damn, dad," I sighed. **"That was something I needed to handle on my own."**

"I tried to tell him that," my mother said in the background.

"And like I told her," my dad let out, **"if I let a nigga live after trying to take out my child, I'm less than the man y'all know me to be. It's handled and that's that. Focus on moving forward and handling yo other business."**

"How'd you even find...nevermind."

"Yeah, nothing's changed. I'll tell you this though, y'all better appreciate having Dudas on the team. I love you, daughter."

"I love you too, dad. I'll talk to y'all."

"Uh huh."

I ended the call and tossed my phone on the counter out of pure frustration. I appreciated my father stepping behind me, but I needed that kill for my own closure. I wanted to look the shooter in his eyes as I emptied a clip into him. And now my dad had taken the fun out of it. Then he mentioned Dudas which let me know he had pulled some kind of strings to carry out the plan. They didn't even bother throwing me in the loop.

"You ready?" Money asked, standing in the entryway of the bathroom door.

I turned to face him, leaning up against the sink. "Did my dad tell you he found the shooter?"

"No bullshit? He told you that just now?"

"Yeah. Along with telling me the person was no longer with us."

"That's what the fuck I'm talkin' bout, Dough!" He boasted. "That's how I'm gon' step about our kid. Laying niggas the fuck down bout mine."

"I wish you would stop doing that."

"Watchu mean, doing what?"

"Talkin' bout kids that you know I can't have." Picking up my phone, I walked around him and out of the bathroom to my closet to put my shoes on.

"That bothers you?" He asked from behind me.

"Yes, it does. It's like, why keep putting it in the atmosphere when you know it's only a set up for failure."

"I want you to bring my mama back and leave the cancer."

"What?" I tuned to face him.

"You heard me. Since you seem to be God, bring my mama back cancer free. We miss her like a motherfucka, and I want her back." I checked his face and there was no smile or smirk present. He was dead serious.

"I'm not in no way tryna play God, Money. I'm telling you a scientific fact."

"Nah, you telling me what a motherfucka told you that you believed and holding onto it as if it's the holy grail. Only the big man upstairs got the last say so, mama." Stepping closer so that he was in front of me, he lifted my chin and placed two kisses on my lips. "I'll be in the car. Hurry up, I don't wanna be late."

He left the room, leaving me to ponder his words. I wanted so bad to have the same optimism as he and my mother did, but I knew I couldn't handle that kind of disappointment. So, rather than pity myself, I put my shoes on, grabbed a light jacket and my purse, and left the house.

"You good?" Money asked once I got in the passenger seat.

"Yes. Gimmie kiss." He leaned over and kissed me.

"I love you."

"I love you, too, Montez."

"I know. Let's go let these niggas know that the third member of 3LW is back." He smiled and kissed the back of my hand.

"Nigga, please." I punched his arm. "How you gon' go from Destiny's Child to 3LW."

"Aight, aight, damn. I ain't never met a group of women that wanna be Ruff Ryders so damn bad."

"Montez, shut uuppp." I chuckled and shook my head. I had really consented to a relationship with this fool. This shit was sure to be an experience.

Chapter Thirteen

MORAE

A WEEK HAD PASSED SINCE I POPPED UP ON DEREK AND threatened him with his mother's life. Luckily for her, he complied and followed my instructions without incident. After Dudas confirmed that the charges had in fact been dropped, I released Derek's mother the next day. I didn't let her go immediately because I wanted him to sit in the bullshit he'd created. She was dropped off late night to his front door, blindfolded with a note pinned to her shirt.

I watched from my car as he opened the door, and she fell into his arms. The note read in a jest that it was in his best interest to walk light moving forward. And that there were no second chances with me. Holding his mother close, his head swiveled from left to right. I started up my car and drove slowly pass his house, making sure to flash my lights during my exit. I wanted him on edge. I wanted that nigga scared of his own shadow.

The tactic seemed to work because we hadn't had any issues since then. I made sure to check in with Dudas to see if Derek's mother had reported her kidnapping and he hadn't heard anything. Clearly, she was shaken up enough. All I wanted was for motherfuckas to stay on their side of the street and I'd stay on mine. Once I assured my father that the situation was handled, he let Monk Man come back home.

He didn't release him without an earful for the both of us, though. Along with his lecture, he set out a few conditions. He let me know that should any problems arise going forward and he was last to know, he'd be sure to make us feel it. I didn't need him to go into detail as to what that meant. I only promised that it would never happen again.

"You heading out?" Monk Man asked, entering my room and taking a seat on the edge of my bed.

He was happy to be back home, and it showed by the way he found his way in my room more than once since he got back.

"Yeah. I got a meeting with The Table. It shouldn't be too long, though. You need something?"

"Can I go?"

I slid my feet into a pair of sneakers and bent over to lace them. "Go where?"

"To the meeting. I ain't got shit else to do. Dad had a nigga over there working this whole week. I feel like he was waiting to get me over there just to do some shit."

"Aww, he missed you. Dad getting up there in age so those Sunday dinners ain't gon' be enough for him. We gotta make some other plans. As far as you going to the meeting, though..." I thought about it for a minute. I didn't have a problem with him tagging along because Monk Man knew how to conduct himself. I didn't know what the meeting would be about though, only that Hogany had requested everyone's attendance. "Text Hogany, and if she says you good then you can ride."

"Bet." He pulled out his phone and typed away. "She said, yeah." He stood up and went to leave out. "Hey, have you heard from Paris?"

I grabbed my Cartier bracelets off the dresser and put them on as I thought about his question. I'd been doing so much running that it hadn't crossed my mind that I hadn't spoken to Paris since I left Derek's shop. "Nah, I haven't."

His face was puzzled. "Oh. Damn, so you really not fuckin' with her like that no more?"

"I don't know. Why you asked if I heard from her, though? Walk with me. I'm not tryna be late for this meeting, so I need you to get a move on." I hit the light for my room and grabbed my phone and purse, closing my bedroom door behind me.

"Cause I wanted to hit her up to see if I could see my lil' man, DJ. I didn't wanna just hit her phone given the circumstances, ya know."

I nodded. "I get it and that's good that you're mindful in that way. However, what me and her got going on don't have nothing to do with the relationship y'all built outside of me. And you know she never believed that bullshit her bd said about you. If it makes you feel any better, I'll hit her for you."

"Thanks, sis."

"No problem, scary ass," I joked.

"Maann, please. Let me go throw something on, gimmie twenty minutes."

"Real funny, nigga. Make it fifteen or I'm gone."

"Wow, a five-minute difference."

"Now four, cause you still standing here." He turned and jogged off to his room.

My offer to call Paris for him was to my benefit as well. This was the longest we'd gone without speaking and while I was wrapped up in my business, it didn't mean she hadn't crossed my mind. I missed DJ, too. I'd gone from seeing him almost every day to not having any communication. And though it hadn't been a long period of time, it was long enough for me. I dialed her number on my phone and the phone rang once before going to voicemail. I wasn't sure if she sent me to voicemail because she didn't wanna talk or if she was busy. Whatever the reason, I didn't call back.

"Aight, I'm ready." I nodded in approval of Monk Man's attire which was a simple Essentials sweatsuit and a pair of Yeezy 500's.

"You strapped?" He lifted his shirt to show the butt of his gun. "Let's ride, gangsta."

I LET MONK MAN CONNECT HIS PHONE FOR MUSIC AS WE drove to the warehouse and instantly regretted it soon as he started playing that drill shit. These lil' niggas were just angry as hell and ready to gun shit down at any given time. Now, I didn't have a problem with them standing on their shit but giving a play by play in the music was just asinine in my opinion. And most of the record labels could give a fuck... a hit was a hit. Drill had Gen Z in a chokehold, Monk Man included.

I turned the music down as we turned into the warehouse. "Remind me not to let you connect yo phone in my shit no more," I said, pulling around back and parking.

Monk Man chuckled. "What?"

"Nothing, just remind me. Come on." We got out at the same time, and I checked my surroundings before walking to the back door.

Like my dad had taught him, Monk Man walked behind me to watch my back. Growing up, my brothers were taught to move this way if it was just me and one of them and if all three of them were around, two on the side of me and one behind. My dad said they were to protect his princess in his absence. Neither of them deviated from that.

Typing in my special code, the door unlocked, and we entered the warehouse. We walked through two empty rooms before reaching the meeting area where Hogany, Money, and Tiffany sat at the conference table.

"Hey, sis, they let you out?" I spoke to Tiffany, making my way over to her.

"Finally, shit. Y'all were having fun without me." She stood from her seat and hugged me.

"Ahhh, not really."

"Hey, Tiff," Monk Man spoke, following me. "You look good."

"Bruh, don't getcho lil' ass beat," Money threatened next to her.

"Ignore him," Tiff waved her hand at Money. "Thank you, Monk Man." She embraced him and Monk Man smirked, fucking with our brother.

"Wassup, y'all," Hogany greeted. We did the same and took a seat with Monk Man opting to stand along with Money.

"Everybody on the way?"

"Yep. Everybody that's supposed to be here. We're gonna have a quick meet with someone before the collective gets here, though."

"Who's that?" Tiff inquired.

"Santana."

"Really?" I questioned. I was glad that she told us before he walked in.

"Yeah. I was waiting for Tiff to be back in the building before bringing him in to officially meet the two of you. It'll be part two of his preliminary screening. Now, Money, I've kept in mind how you felt about him, but we've had some recent developments that are making me look at the situation differently. Any objections to this meet?" She met each of our eyes and I was the first to speak.

"If you let him in up till this point to where you want us to meet him, let alone at this location, you already screened him and feel he's on the up and up, am I right?"

"For the most part. I'm not fully convinced though and that's where my team comes in."

"How long before he get here?" Tiff asked.

Hogany checked her watch and answered. "He should be pulling up now."

"Cool." Tiff reached behind her and set her .45 on the table. I smirked. "After Pete, we ain't taking no chances. Anything feel funny, niggas gotta meet Uncle Charles at the motherfuckin' crossroads."

"Welcome back, gangsta," I said, and she nodded.

"Glad to be back."

"Money, he just pulled up. You and Monk Man go let him in," Hogany instructed. As they left the room, she turned to me and Tiff. "Anything off about this nigga, call it as you see it. We not here to make him comfortable. This is a business meeting, so we'll be setting aside the fact that he is my brother."

"Ahh, bitch, he yo brother now?" Tiffany let out and I snickered.

"You know what I mean, heffa."

"I guess," Tiff replied. "I got it, though. I wasn't taking it easy anyway."

"Neither am I," I added. I took out my gun and sat it down just as Tiff had.

"Well, let's get into some gangsta shit," Mahogany said as Santana walked in with Monk Man in front of him and Money bringing up the rear. "Santana, you've met Tiff, this is Morae, Money, and Monk Man." She made introductions and Santana nodded at us.

I almost expected him to hold his hand out for a handshake and I was glad to see that he hadn't. I would have only taken it for him trying too hard. He glanced down at the guns set in front of us and smirked while raising his shirt.

"Good thing I never leave home without mine." He flashed the butt of his gun.

"It would be useless if we didn't allow you to bring it in here," I said. "Tell me, do you think you'd be able to get to it faster than I can get to mine?"

"Shiidd, we can see."

Monk Man cocked his gun and pointed it to the back of Santana's head. I got up from my seat and invaded his space. "I'll take that." I pulled his gun from his waist and when my hand brushed across his skin, I froze temporarily. Looking up at him, I snapped back quickly and took a step back, placing his gun next to mine.

"We good, young bull," he said to Monk Man who only backed down once I gave him the signal to do so. "Listen, I really ain't the enemy here. I'm just tryna do business."

"How's your business back in Cali?" Tiff asked, sitting up with her hands folded.

"I left it in capable hands."

"So, you left your shit back in Cali where you're *the boss* to come here on a whim to work *under* someone? Your sister at that. That makes sense to you, cause me saying it out loud sounds crazy to me."

Tiff made a valid point. One that I hadn't questioned since he made his appearance. Hogany was quiet, and I'm sure she wanted to know the answer as well.

"Well, if I'm being honest, what I've been doing in Cali has nothing on the foundation The Table has been built on, long before you ladies were put in position." I caught the shade but let it roll off my shoulders. "I move smart, and this is a numbers game. In that, I'm able to keep my operation going in Cali and still maintain a position here at The Table. I'm all about my paper so I'ma make it work regardless. All I need is an opening and shit gon' go."

"Why'd you wait to expose Pete?" I asked, wanting to know his reasoning.

"I wanted to make sure I had all the evidence first. As you probably know, she," he pointed to Mahogany, "don't really fuck with me. It was bad enough that I was around during the shooting that happened, now here I am associating with a nigga on the team who just so happened to be plotting. There wouldn't have been room for error, so I had to make sure to have all my ducks in a row."

"I assume because you did your good deed you expect Pete's spot at The Table?"

"Wrong. I ain't tryna fill no nigga shoes. Especially a nigga with that kind of mark on his name. I want my own seat, with a clean slate."

"I'll do you one better," Mahogany spoke up. "We're expanding and the West Coast is first on our list. If you wanna be a part of this, those spots that you currently have need to be under *this* umbrella. Meaning, you'll no longer be a separate entity. You'll operate under The Table with your own territory."

He folded his arms, putting his hand up to his chin, in deep thought. "What's the split?"

"60/40 my way, until I see what you can do. If you can make the keys I lay on you disappear like magic in a timely fashion, it'll be an even split. And them bitches come in hot, so you'll never have to worry bout a drought."

"What do you say, Santana? You ready to be a big timer?" I asked in a condescending tone.

"It's good to be a part of the family business," he said with a smile. Oddly, I found myself smiling too but quickly made my lips form a straight line before anyone could notice.

"Sounds good," Mahogany said and stood from her seat. "I don't do fuck ups and I'm not fond of second chances. My respect is earned, not given. The object of this partnership is to make money and a lot of it. Before you bring your issues to me, you go through Mo. She's an extension of me. Understand that where we stand as blood relatives means nothing to me when it comes down to it. As I've mentioned before, I don't know you and you don't know me. Business is business and I'm gonna deal with you just as I deal with everybody else that holds a position in this organization."

"I don't expect anything less," he retorted.

"The guys have arrived," I announced.

"Thanks, Mo. Money, let them in please. Santana, you can take the seat next to Mo. Go head and give him his gun." I slid it to him, and he caught it in his hand.

"Thanks, shorty," he said with a wink. Ignoring him, I watched as the men filed in.

One by one, they took their seats, and everyone sat up in anticipation for what Mahogany had to say. Each person knew that if a meeting was ever called before reup then it was important.

"Good evening fellas, thanks for coming out," Hogany greeted, while walking back to her seat. The men said their hellos and gave her their undivided attention. "Two things on the agenda tonight and the first one, I'm gonna get out of the way pretty quickly. Pete is no longer with us. Last I checked, he was on his way to hell and had no plans on returning. What brought about his sudden exit you ask? Well, the answer is pretty simple, you fuck with me, I end you." I eyed every face in the room, and no one said a word, nor did they react. "Next order of business, we're setting up for expansion and Santana here will be aiding in that process. Will expansion affect the way we move going forward? Yes, it will. Will it be in a negative way? Only if you let it. Everyone is still responsible for their own shit. Should there be a change during expansion that directly affects your paper, that's something you need to speak with me about. Expansion means less visibility for Mo here. With her being head lieutenant, you all know that she oversees all territories. Which means, she'll be overseeing the new territory as we get it up and running."

Santana and I locked eyes, and he winked at me again. I didn't know what that shit meant but he needed to chill. Hogany hadn't spoken to me about going to Cali, but it wasn't surprising that it was something she'd thought of.

"Will the number for product still be the same?" Briscoe asked.

"Yep," she answered quickly without even looking at him. "Along with what I already mentioned, expansion usually means business is doing well, in case anyone was wondering. Are there any other questions?"

"Whose taking over Pete's spot?" Briscoe posed another question.

Knowing it was prime real estate, I could see why he was ready to jump on it.

"It's up for grabs to the highest bidder. You wanna put something on it?"

"We can talk numbers."

"See me after the meeting. Fellas," she turned back to the collective, "when the time comes for Mo to go, you'll report directly to Money. If there's no further questions, the meeting is adjourned. Thank you."

Everyone got up from their seats and made their exit. Money, Tiff, and Monk Man talked amongst themselves while Hogany and Briscoe left the room. That left me seated with Santana who decided to hang around for reasons unknown.

"Don't you have a family to get home to?" I asked, taking out my phone to text Paris. "Ain't no need in you sitting around, we said you're in."

"Why y'all so damn mean? Y'all don't have a soft side to y'all?"

I turned so that I was fully facing him. "We do. It's usually reserved for close family or the person we're fucking."

"You know this gangsta shit you got going on is a turn on, right?" I smirked at his bluntness. "We should probably work on getting along now since we gotta be around each other when we make it to my side of town."

"Santana, I ain't gotta do shit but stack my bread, stay black, and die. Trust me, if I can help it, our interactions will be minimal. I provide the work, make sure shit is moving in accordance with The Table's standards, and you do your part."

He leaned in close to me and I didn't budge. Yeah, Santana was fine and all but that shit only got you but so far with me. "I'ma see you soon, Mo." He did the opposite of what I thought he was gonna do. Smooth shit like that, I could fuck with. "Y'all be easy," he said to everyone as he left out.

My eyes lingered in his direction a little too long because I caught Tiffany watching me watch him. The small smirk on her face didn't go unnoticed. I thought I could get away with ignoring her and putting my head down in my phone but in true Tiffany fashion, she couldn't let me slide and slid her ass over to me.

"So, how you feel?" She asked, taking a seat beside me.

"About?"

She cocked her head to the side. "About Santana. And I'm asking from a business standpoint."

"What other standpoint would you be asking from, Tiff?"

"You wanna go there?"

"Nope," I responded, in an effort to drop the subject before she could drag it. Knowing Tiff, she couldn't wait to point out some shit that she thought she saw. "I think Santana is gonna be a pain in the ass but his confidence and the fact that he doesn't back down are qualities of a money maker."

"Agreed. We shall see how it plays out, though. He seems quite fond of you."

"See, here you go. Let me get outta here. Let's ride, Monk Man." I got up and walked around her.

"Oh, it's cool when you do it, it's a problem when I do it, fuck it." She quoted the Finesse2tymes lyrics, making me laugh.

"You're annoying."

"Whateva. Monk Man, you ride with your brother and me and my good sis gonna ride together." Catching up to me, she put her arm in mine.

"So annoying."

She stuck her tongue out at me. "Yeah, yeah. Let me check on Hogany then we can head out."

Just as she mentioned Hogany's name, her and Briscoe reentered the conference room. I assumed their conversation didn't go well by their body language. I wasn't surprised seeing as most of their one-on-one interactions ended that way these days.

"You straight?" Tiff asked.

"Yeah, I'm good. I have somewhere to be, and I don't need an escort tonight, Tiff. I'm playing it light. Monk Man, come with me to my car. I gotta show you something." She proceeded to walk out, and Monk Man followed.

I glanced over at Briscoe and shook my head. "The hell you do now? Can't get right, headass."

"That's y'all problem. Y'all always thinkin' it's me. Mahogany got some shit with her, too," he let out frustrated.

"Nigga, even if that was the case, you've *been* on one for a while now," Tiffany jumped in.

"Maann, I ain't bout to sit here and defend myself in a situation y'all don't know enough about. Mo," he looked to me, "I'm gonna need to reup by the end of the week. I'll hit yo phone."

"Chill out on your tone with my lady, my nigga," Money spoke up. He was so quiet, for a minute, I forgot he was still in the room.

He and Briscoe locked eyes a few seconds and Briscoe snickered. "Nigga, go head with that shit."

"Alriiight, meeting was adjourned a few minutes ago. How bout we all go our way?" I suggested. Before their little exchange became a thing, I shut it down. "I'll catch you soon, Briscoe," I said, dismissing him.

Making sure that we secured the warehouse, we all went outside where we met Mahogany and Monk Man in the parking lot talking next to her car. She handed him something that he pocketed and nodded. I tapped Tiff and we headed in Hogany's direction while Monk Man headed towards Money's car.

"Mo, I want you to keep a close eye on Santana for me, okay," Hogany said. "I'll be watching from afar but being that y'all are gonna work closely together, you'll have better insight."

"I got you. How long you think its gonna take to set up in Cali?"

"Not long at all. I've already done my research. He only has a few spots out there. You'll go out there, put everything in motion as far as letting everyone know that they will be operating under The Table umbrella, and then once the product lands, it'll sell itself."

"You good?" Tiff asked her.

"You asked me that already. I said I was, remember?"

"I know what you said *verbally*, but your body language is another story. I'll leave it alone, though."

"I have a suggestion," I said with my finger up.

"Go head."

"You need to be fucked."

"Girl, what?" She giggled.

"I agree," Tiffany concurred. "All work and no play, make the cobwebs stay."

"Wait a minute now, bitch. Ain't no cobwebs down there," Hogany argued.

"Yeah, but it's been a while, I'm sure." I spoke like I knew what was going on in her bedroom. Mahogany was so damn secretive at times; we only knew if we pried the information out of her or if she volunteered. "Go link up with, Mr. Blackstone." I changed my voice, mocking Justice.

"Y'all on me. Back it up, back it up, back it up. And Mo, while you in my business, how bout you go check on Paris? She ain't been to the club and I haven't pressured her because she did call a few days ago to tell me she needed a mental pause."

"I'm gonna slide through there, now. I tried to call her but she ain't answer." I felt bad now.

"I think that's a good idea. I'm gone and congrats, Tiff."

"On what?" Tiffany was confused.

"Money said y'all having a baby."

"No, he didn't," she refuted.

Mahogany laughed. "Yes, he did. Text me when y'all make it home. And Mo, let me know what's going on with, P. Love y'all."

"Love you, too." I laughed at Tiffany's facial expression as Hogany pulled off. Putting my arm in hers as she'd done me, I put my head on her shoulder. "Sooo, you want a boy or girl?"

ON THE RIDE TO PARIS' HOUSE, I THOUGHT ABOUT HER calling out of work. That had never been a thing for her and the fact that Mahogany hadn't mentioned it until tonight meant that she asked her not to. Paris was all about her paper so her calling out for a day, let alone a few days was a tell-tale sign of where she was mentally. I may not have been concerned before, but I was now. Pulling onto her street, I cut my music down.

"When's the last time you spoke to P?" Tiff asked from the

passenger seat. She'd been quiet the whole time, giving me the space needed to think.

"When I went to her bd's shop and threatened him."

"Oh, how was her reaction to that and did you get the results you were looking for?"

"Yeah. The charges were dropped, and we haven't heard anything since. And her reaction was that of concern, for me not him."

"I'm sure it was. She adores you."

I said nothing in response as I parked across the street from her apartment building. Again, I dialed her number, and it went to voice-mail. I still had a key to her crib but after having not spoken to her in a week, I didn't think it was cool for me to just barge into her place.

"Can you try to call her from your phone?"

"Yeah, hold on." She took her phone from her purse and dialed. Placing the phone on speaker, she sat it in her lap. Just like with my call, she got the voicemail. "Just go up. I'll wait right here for you. The worst that could happen is she don't answer the door, or she answers and closes it in your face."

"Wow, what a good pep talk," I said sarcastically. Unlocking my door, I pushed it open.

"Hey, I do what I can," Tiff hollered from her window as I walked around the car.

It was late and not an ideal time to be checking on someone, but I just wanted to make sure she was good. Two cars passed and as the crosswalk became clear for me to cross, I saw Paris emerge from her building with a dude walking beside her. From what I could see with my perfect 20/20 vision, they appeared to be holding hands. I watched them walk briskly to a Lexus Coupe and the door was opened for Paris to get in the passenger side. Just as quickly as she slid in, the dude slid into the driver's side and peeled off.

I turned and walked back to my car, biting the inside of my cheek. I wasn't pissed about her being with a nigga but to blatantly ignore my calls when I was genuinely concerned was what blew me.

"Was that...?" Tiff asked once I pulled the driver's side door open.

"Yep. Am I taking you home?" I spoke, nonchalantly. As she went to respond, my phone rang. Seeing Paris' aunt's number on the caller id was unexpected. I started not to answer it but figured I should since calling me was something she rarely did. I slid the green arrow across the screen for the call to connect.

"Hello."

"Hey, Morae. I'm sorry to call you so late, love, but I wanted to see if you've heard from Paris today."

I looked over at Tiff then back at the phone. **"Umm, no, I haven't."**

"Shoot. I've been trying to get her on the phone since she told me she was coming to get DJ, but it keeps going to voicemail. I'll try her again. Thank you, honey."

"Wait, Ms. Reece," I called out before she could end the call. **"When's the last time you heard from her?"**

"Maybe about two hours ago. She said she was out running some errands and that she was going to stop home before coming here."

Puzzled, I looked to Tiff again whose face shared my thoughts.

"Hello, you still there?"

"Yes... yes, I'm still here. Umm, I'll try to reach out to her. Maybe she fell asleep." I didn't want to let on that I thought something was wrong, although at this point, I *felt* something was.

"Well, alright. I'm gonna go head and put DJ to bed. Just let me know if you hear anything before I do, and I'll do the same."

"Okay, no problem." The call ended and I sat my phone down in my lap.

"Why didn't you tell her that you saw P?"

I stared straight ahead. "Cause then I'd have to tell her that there was a *strong* possibility that I just witnessed her niece's kidnapping."

Chapter Fourteen

SANTANA

When I got the official invite to a meeting at The Table, I knew I had solidified my spot. Mahogany could've met with me at my hotel, her club, our mama's crib, hell even at Ihop, but she chose to link me at headquarters. I pulled up to the meeting in true Santana fashion. Cocky as ever and on my shit. Seeing the guns sitting directly in front of her crew didn't phase me. It was an intimidation tactic, and I wasn't easily intimidated. I showed my shit to let them know that I was on that if it came down to it.

Even when Morae pulled the gun off my hip, I still felt a sense of security. It may have had everything to do with the way her skin brushed up against mine when she grabbed it. She was a bad ass chocolate mama. Skin looked soft as fuck and the dead look in her eyes made her even more attractive for some reason. I loved the way she conducted herself although like with my sister, the hard exterior made it so that people were either afraid to get close to them or didn't bother.

Either way, I was interested in learning more about her as the time presented itself. The timing couldn't have been better for the invite. My circle was starting to get antsy. Renee wanted a timeline as to when things would start moving, Razor had moved the product I'd given him, and I had my pops on my neck wanting to know my every move.

I was able to keep Renee at bay by reassuring her that the train was moving and she had nothing to worry about. She knew I was Mr. Make-ItHappen, so the only reason I could think of as to why she was so adamant about it was solely due to her being out of her comfort zone. Other than the shopping and sightseeing, she'd expressed that the fast-paced New York streets wasn't her scene. I knew she'd find comfort in knowing we were able to return home.

Thinking about Mahogany's proposition for my blocks to operate under The Table was a no brainer. I saw the bigger picture and figured I'd have to give up something minor in order to attain something major. Hell, after the dirt I'd thrown on Pete's name, I wasn't sure how far I'd go to be on top.

I had to be mindful, though. My sister was fucking ruthless. The way she put a bullet in Pete's head without a second thought, there was no doubt in my mind that I could be on the other end of her gun if I moved wrong, or worse, my *true intentions* were exposed. Hence, the reason why I showed up with the dude in my trunk. It was me pledging my allegiance to The Table and she went for it. I popped him, sent the evidence as requested, and that was that.

Leaving the warehouse, I decided to pull up on my mother. We hadn't had a one on one yet, and seeing as I was two steps forward with Mahogany, I figured getting some one-on-one time with her would be good. Scrolling through our text messages, I searched for her address. Finding it, I plugged it into my GPS. Gearing up for the ride, I dialed Razor's number. I wanted to tap in with him for an update. It was important that I stayed in his ear and kept him in the loop, knowing he had the tendency to go rogue at times.

The phone rang twice before going to voicemail. Hanging up, I went to dial again and an incoming call from him came through.

"Yo, what's the word," he said once the call connected.

"We in, my nigga!" I let out with more excitement than I intended.

"About goddamn time. That's what the fuck I'm talkin' bout, dawg! You had a nigga worried for a minute there."

"Nigga, I told you I was gon' make shit happen. You just had to give me room to work my ones and twos."

"Yeah, I hear you. You know how I am, though. When I'm on, I gotta go."

"Shit same goes for me. Some situations take a little bit of time and finessing, though. This was one of those situations. I get how you're used to us operating which is why I laid that brick on you."

When I gave Razor the kilo of coke, I didn't ask for anything in return, but he made sure to give me a cut from whatever his profit was. I had no way of knowing whether the cut was a solid amount or not, but Razor was my boy and had never snaked me. He just didn't have the face for that kind of shit.

"Yeah, and I made it do what it do," he replied.

"Fa sho. Like I said though, we on. And what's even better is we get to do this shit in our own backyard."

"What you mean?"

Before I could respond, I heard a female ask for something to drink in the background. I picked up on the hesitance in her tone. Almost as if she was *scared* to speak. Razor responded, telling her to wait.

"Who dat?" I questioned.

"A little friend of mine. Don't worry bout that, though. What's this you talkin' bout with our backyard?"

He hadn't mentioned linking anyone since we got here, but then again, I would've been surprised if he did. All the years I'd known Razor, he'd never been in a relationship, let alone talk to anyone for more than a few weeks. I was sure he didn't come to New York to find a woman.

"They're expanding," I spoke. "The operation is moving out West and she wants me to take the reins."

"So, you'll be working under her?"

"Nah, nigga. I'm working alongside her."

"Well alright then, let's get this shit crackin'."

"Damn, right. My nigga, the money we bout to touch is gonna make this whole shit worthwhile."

"Yeah, it *better* be. I would hate to have to go with the alternative." The last part he said under his breath, but I heard it loud and clear.

"**What's the alternative?**" I questioned, wanting him to speak his mind.

"**Huh?**" He faked confusion.

Deciding not to press the issue, I left it in the air to float around.

"**Nothing, bruh. We'll be heading back home sooner than you think. It'll give you time to decide what you wanna do witcho lil' friend,**" I joked.

He chuckled, only there wasn't any lightness to it to show that he found the joke remotely funny.

"**Yeah. I'll tie up my loose ends before then. Let me get off this phone though and tend to this business.**"

"**Aight.**" He hung up and the conversation replayed in my head. I knew Razor. He was up to something and whatever it was, he better hope it didn't fuck up what I had been working overtime to establish.

WALKING INTO MY MOTHER'S HOUSE, THE SMELL OF CHICKEN frying hit my nostrils immediately. She didn't mention cooking when I called to let her know I wanted to stop by. I was glad she did though cause my stomach was growling. We'd been eating out since we touched down in New York and there was nothing like a home cooked meal. I rubbed my hands like Birdman as she closed the door behind me.

"Yo hungry ass," my mother commented, shaking her head. "Come on in the kitchen."

I smiled and followed her. "Why you cooking so late, ma?" I asked her as we turned the corner and entered her chef's kitchen.

That nigga Coolie had shit set out for my mother. My first visit here with Renee and Asia, she gave us a tour after dinner. The house was massive, the outside did it no justice. The six-bedroom, five-bathroom house equipped with beauty suite and theatre may have been just too much house for my mother. Knowing Coolie growing up though, I knew that when it came to his family, he spared no expense which was why he always got my respect.

She shrugged her shoulders. "I couldn't sleep. When Coolie is heavy on my mind, I get up and cook one of his favorite meals. He should be calling soon. What brings you by?" She pulled the crispy, golden chicken out of the cast iron pot and sat it on a wire rack for it to drain.

In my head I thought that shit was just too bougie but said nothing about it. "I just came from a meeting at The Table with Mahogany and her people." I took a seat at the kitchen island and placed my phone face down in front of me.

"Oh, how was that?" She seemed surprised.

"It was cool. They gave me a real warm welcome."

She turned to me with a smirk on her face. "Who drew on you first, Tiff or Mo?"

"Shit, both." We both shared a laugh, and she shook her head. "How you know?"

"My girls don't play, baby. They on go when it comes to The Table, and they will put a nigga down behind your sister." I watched as she pulled a new pack of Dixie paper plates out the cabinet and placed a few chicken wings on it. Placing the plate in front of me, she leaned on the island.

"I just knew you were gonna put the chicken on fine china."

"I could've, but why make more dishes? And are you tryna lowkey call me bougie, boy?" She stood back and placed her hands on her hips.

I grinned and picked up a wing. "Nah, not like that. I just took notice of some things that's all. Ain't no big thang."

"Mmmhmm. Just because it's been years since we've been in each other's presence don't mean I ain't yo same mama. No matter what bullshit yo father put in yo head. What you want to drink? And I'm out of Kool-Aid." She took a shot at me, letting me know she was offended by what I thought about her. That, on top of what she said about my pops.

"Come on, ma. I didn't mean to make you feel no type of way. I'll take a bottle of water, please." She went to the fridge and out of the four brands of water I could see she had inside, she grabbed the Poland Spring.

"Damn, a nigga can't even get the Essentia joint?" I asked, taking the Poland Spring and cracking the top.

"Nah, smart ass. You lucky I ain't giving you tap but that's filtered so it would be the same as that Poland you bought to drink." She took her spot back at the island and watched me eat in silence for a few minutes. "Was I a bad mom?"

Her question came out of the blue and made me sit the chicken down on the plate before answering. "Nah, you weren't," I answered truthfully. "You were a great mom. You still are from what I can see. And a great grandmother."

"So, why did you choose to stay with your dad? Were you not happy here with me and Coolie? Did I miss something as far as what you needed? Here," she handed me a napkin to clean my hands.

"Real shit, ma, I just wanted to be able to run the streets and create my own path. There was nothing wrong with you or Coolie. I had it good with y'all. I never wanted for nothing. Shit, y'all anticipated the wants before I asked. And by the time, I got around to it, I already had it. Only thing y'all couldn't or refused to give me was access to the game. Yeah, I rode around with Coolie and saw him handle business, but he was never on the front lines because in his position he didn't have to be. Pops, on the other hand, was in the thick of that shit. It was fascinating to me, and he had no problem with me being out there with him."

"In other words, you wanted a freedom that you feel we refused to provide?" She questioned for clarity.

"Yeah, pretty much."

"Has it ever crossed your mind that there was a reason that Coolie had you see the game from a bird's eye view rather than throwing you headfirst in it?"

"Yeah. Cause he didn't want me out on the block. He used to explain that to me all the time when I would take rides with him."

"Baby boy, you heard the talks, but I can tell you *never* took in the lesson. A true boss ain't gon' have his successor manning the corners. You weren't meant to be the nigga that stands on the block and serves or even a lieutenant for that matter. You were being groomed to have the head seat at The Table. And you may not like the way this sounds, but your mother gon' always keep it A1 witchu. Your father has been in *the same* position for years and while he's made a name for himself and gained some respect, a name ain't shit if you don't know how to move."

I let her words sink in and as I went to take a private trip down memory lane of the times spent with Coolie, the sounds of Luther Vandross' "If This World Were Mine" played.

"I'll be back," she said, leaving me in the kitchen and alone with my thoughts.

The realization of every word Coolie spoke to me when we took our drives hit me at one time. I was too young and in a rush to grow up to get it then. Moms was right. I had heard the talks, but the lessons had gone over my head. And now, here I was trying to claim a title that could've been mine to begin with. As the doubt of pushing forward with my plan started to sink in, my phone vibrated. Picking it up, my pops name was clear on the screen. What were the odds that he'd be calling at this very moment.

"Waddup, pop?" I greeted.

"Shit, you tell me. I haven't heard from you since our last conversation. I'm checking in on you."

I heard him subtly ask, what the fuck I had going on. **"I'm building, pop."**

"And how's that coming along?"

"Moving in the right direction. I'll be back on the West Coast soon."

"Nigga, that wasn't the plan. What yo ass done went up there and did? You let them throw that, *we are family* bullshit yo way?" His chastising was nothing new. He had my back, but ultimately, he wanted me to move the way he saw fit. That didn't work for me.

"Maann," I let out and paused once my mother returned to the kitchen with her phone to her ear.

"You good?" She asked, eyeing my phone.

"Yeah. Chopping it up with pops." I told the truth to avoid suspicion.

"Oh, okay," she responded. **"He's on a call, baby,"** I heard her say into the phone as she exited the kitchen again.

"Why you ain't say you was at your mom's house?" My pops asked.

"Cause I don't report my every move to you, pop. Come on now with that shit." We hadn't been on the phone a few minutes and

I was getting irritated. I wasn't sure if it was because of him questioning me or the conversation with my mom that was on my head.

"I see what it is," he let out. **"You went up there and did *exactly* what I thought you were gonna do."**

"And what's that?" Dragging my hand across my face, I let out a sigh of frustration.

"Let your mom and that nigga Coolie get in your head and forget the task at hand. What they do, dangle a little position in the air? Oh, no, I know what they did. They told you that you were family, huh. Nigga, they ain't yo family. Me, Renee, Razor, and Asia is yo family. We the ones that's *been* in the trenches witchu. You losing sight of that?" I couldn't shake the animosity in his tone mixed with pure hatred and jealousy.

"I ain't lose sight of shit," I spat.

"Hmph. You could've fooled me. I'ma let you go and have your family time, though. Know this, what you ain't willing to do, it's a motherfucka out there willing to take it to the furthest extent to get it done." The line went dead.

I flexed my hand open and close and bit the inside of my jaw. This nigga had me .38 hot, talkin' all that bullshit.

"Santana." I turned slightly towards my mother's voice. "Whatever he put in your head, you better think it through and consider everything before you execute. Certain shit you just can't come back from, son."

Chapter Fifteen

RAZOR

"Damn, girl, you see a nigga on the phone and shit, that's rude as hell. And didn't I just give you some water?" I questioned the baddie in front of me.

She sat in a chair with her hands and feet bound and a scarf covered her eyes, preventing her from seeing her surroundings. Her request for water was the first few words she'd uttered since I picked her up. I half expected her to at least ask who I was and what I wanted with her, but she hadn't said either. I chalked it up to the shock of me catching her as she left her apartment building and putting the Bulldog to her side. Or maybe she'd been in this situation before. Whatever the case, her pretty ass was a mute.

"No," she spoke up, "you offered me water and seeing how you have me blindfolded and I can't see what's being given to me, there was no way I was drinking anything from you."

"So, are you asking me to take the blindfold off?"

"Just so I can see the water and take a few sips. If you can't do that, then I'm good. I'm taking a chance by even letting you do that."

I smirked, even though she couldn't see me. "Girl, what kind of man do you think I am? Why would I do something to your water?" I pushed the conversation. Leaning back against the off-white wall, I waited to hear her answer. We were in a hotel in Newark. It was a fucked-up area that I was sure no one would come looking for her in.

She scoffed. "I know I can't see, but I damn sure can feel. My hands and feet are tied, and you forced me into your car at gunpoint not too long ago. It's safe to say that you're a fucked up individual. What kind of man do I think you are? Nigga, a *sick* one. A *bitch ass* nigga. A *desperate ass* nigga. Oh, and I just know you ugly. Prolly got a lil' dick, too."

"Ay, that's where I draw the line. I ain't ugly, shorty. This dick long and got some weight on it, too. You wanna see it?" I took a step forward and stood on the side of her. I unzipped my jeans to make her think I was about to pull out.

"What are you doing?" Her change in tone let me know that her confidence was slipping a bit. I said nothing in response, wanting her nervous about my next move. "What are you doing?" She asked again.

Glancing down at her chest, I watched it rise and fall in her white V-neck shirt. The bra she wore had pushed her small titties up and I admired the way the titty meat looked as her breathing quickened a little. Something about her cream-colored skin made my dick hard. I had a thing for bitches with the natural glow about themselves. Despite the position I'd put her in, there was no denying my attraction. I had half a mind to pull out and jerk my shit. My ringing phone canceled those thoughts.

Only three people had this number, and they were all important pieces to my puzzle in some kind of way. I had to make sure that I was on point when I answered. Zipping up my pants, I checked the phone and smirked at the name before answering.

"You're a terrible side nigga, you know that," the woman on the other end let out.

I laughed and took a few steps back from my captive. **"Come on, boo. I told you I was out handling business. I wasn't at your beck and call back home, what makes you think shit would change now?"** Noticing a mini fridge in the corner of the room, I opened it to see if there were any complimentary bottles of water inside. Opening the fridge, I quickly closed it. **"Goddamn!"** The smell that came from inside was something unexplainable.

"Don't even worry about it, my spit will hold me over," my captive spoke.

"Seriously, Razor. You don't have time for me, but you got time to be out with the next bitch? You keep showing me that you ain't no different than this nigga."

I shook my head. **"Girl, I'm out handling business, I ain't fuckin' around."** I looked over at the baddie and shifted my hard on. **"Anyway, wassup. You need me for something?"**

"Not anymore, I'll just call my man and see what he's doing." She had an attitude but unlike her dude, I wasn't stunting that shit.

"I guess you didn't get the news yet. I'm sure he'll be home soon."

"Really, so you just gon' ignore what I just said?"

"You want attention and right now I'm handling business."

"Whatever, Razor. Don't call me when you need information either, nigga."

"I'm gonna call and you're gonna pick up. Keep in mind that I ain't the only one with shit to lose out here, Renee. Keep it hot fa me, ma." I ended the call and scrolled my text messages. I needed to reach out to my contact to update him on the mission I'd completed and the update I'd just received from Santana.

While sending my message, a text came through from Renee, pulling the notification bar down, I could see there was a picture downloading. Once it completed, it was a picture of her freshly waxed pussy. I licked my lips and swiped the notification bar back up. She was a trip. Me and Renee had started fucking around during Santana's last bid. It wasn't supposed to be anything, just some fucking here and there to take the edge off. Somewhere along the way, she fell in love with the dick and here we are.

"You can tell Derek that as soon as I'm out of here, I will be going for full custody of my son." I ignored shorty because I didn't know who the hell Derek was. It was apparent that she thought he was behind her being snatched up, so I went with it.

Scrolling back to my messages, I sent the text to my contact.

Me: Say, it look like the boy done finally came through with some results. Say he got the greenlight to set up shop on our side. Looks like he was able to keep up on his end after all.

Money Move: I'm not too convinced. I gotta see it with my own eyes. And keep in mind that him getting his own territory was not what we set out to do. I want the whole fucking organization, Razor.

Me: And I get that. This is a step in the right direction, no?

Money Move: Did you get the girl?

He completely ignored my attempt to see the bright side.

Me: Yeah, her pretty ass sitting right in front me.

I looked up from my phone and licked my lips, admiring the baddie from afar. I'd been given her name but pretty and baddie were fitting so I would refer to her as such.

Money Move: Alright, kill her. And then I have someone else for you to pick up.

Me: Damn, man, you sure?

I really ain't wanna kill shorty. I ain't know this nigga was willing to go this far. And it wasn't that I was above pulling the trigger but killing pretty just didn't make any sense to me. I mean, it made no sense as far as the overall goal.

Money Move: I'm positive. This is a crew
that needs to be dismantled piece by piece.
The woman you currently have is the
girlfriend of the head lieutenant. Understand
we're dealing with women who act like men
but still operate on emotion. We gotta tear
shit down around them which will then leave
the spot open because they'll be too
focused on trying to put their lives back
together. You got it?

Me: Yeah.

Money Move: Good. Get it done. And once
you're finish, turn her phone on. They'll track
her from there.

Me: Aight, I'll hit you once I'm outta here.

I locked my phone and slid it inside of my pants pocket. I silently walked across the room, over to the bed. Picking up one of the dingy pillows, I pulled the Bulldog from my waist. Holding the pillow up in one hand, I pointed the gun with the other. She must've sensed me because her body became stiff.

"Mommy loves you, DJ," she let out before I sent a slug to her head. I hung my head and put the gun away.

Usually, a kill made me feel nothing but killing this woman made me feel a twinge of guilt. I knew I had to shake it, though. Taking her phone from my pocket, I powered it on, and it was flooded with missed texts and calls. Behind the lengthy notification bar, I could see a faint picture of her and a little boy.

"Damn," I said out loud to myself. Placing the phone on her lap, I took my hoodie off and used it to wipe down everything I touched before leaving. Jogging over to the exit to take the steps, my phone vibrated. Checking it there was a message from my contact.

Money Move: Pick up the daughter.

Chapter Sixteen

MAHOGANY

Rolling over in bed and into Justice' arms had me feeling the safest I'd felt since my father had been home. Last night after the meeting, he'd sent me a text inviting me to dinner at his house. What I'd done to deserve such an invitation, at such a late hour, I didn't know but I was happy to accept after the frustrating interaction I had with Briscoe after meeting with The Table. Here I was thinking he wanted to *actually* talk numbers and low and behold, this nigga was looking for me to just hand him over Pete's territory. The fucking audacity of this man just kept getting more and more out of this fucking world.

He reasoned that being that he was top earner, it made sense for him to have the prime real estate because I knew that he'd double my money. He'd let the top earner shit go to his head and I had to quickly bring him down to earth. While he brought in a lot of money, he was no use to me if I couldn't count on him when I needed him the most. I mentioned the highway incident where I couldn't reach him, and he gave me a sorry ass apology with the excuse of him being in a bad signal area. Briscoe didn't know it, but he was looking sorrier in my eyes as the days went by.

I quoted the number I would start at for Pete's territory and told him he could either accept it or build onto it. I wasn't coming down from the number I'd set. I left him standing there and walked back out to the girls. I got the text from Justice just as I made my way back out front. I texted back yes to the invitation and told him to make sure that the food was worth my gas and mileage. His house was an hour away from the warehouse. To say the man could throwdown was an understatement. The food he made was definitely worth the trip.

Thinking about the honey glazed stuffed chicken breast with mashed potatoes and asparagus made my stomach growl.

"You don't think it's too soon for that?" I heard Justice say. I wanted to shrivel up and die, thinking that he thought I'd just passed gas.

"That was my stomach," I said, scared to look up at him. My stomach growling out loud was no better, though.

He chuckled. "I figured as much cause I don't smell anything."

"Oh my God," I let out, mortified. I pulled the sheet over my head, thinking about how I could just slip out of the bed even though he was up. Feeling the sheet lifted, I could see him peek his head underneath it.

"You good, baby," he said with a smile. "How'd you sleep?" He left the sheet over his head so that we were now both under it.

"Really good. Especially knowing you didn't take advantage of me." I looked down at the basketball shorts he'd given me to sleep in and they were still on my body. Rolled twice to stay up on my waist and not tampered with.

He chuckled. "Girl, you a trip. I'm sure it's worth the wait and when you give it to me, I'ma be *the last* nigga you give it to so I really ain't trippin'. How was the food?"

"Good as hell! You a chef on the low, ain't you?"

"Nah, but I am my mother's only child. She made sure that I could cook. Said she never wanted me to have to depend on a woman to feed me."

I nodded. "I like that. Luckily for you, I can actually burn. So, you'll be in good hands."

"Oh, you fuckin' wit me?" He asked with that smirk that I'd come to love to see.

"Ummm, I'm in this bed, ain't I? Remember when you weren't

comfortable with me knowing where you laid your head?" I reminded him of what he'd told me at my club.

"Yeah, I remember. I also sleep with this." He reached under his pillow and pulled out a .38 special. "You know, just in case you got to tweaking out in this bitch."

"Respect," I said, reaching under the pillow I slept on and pulling out my .380. "Trust is hard to come by these days."

"You know what, I can fuck witchu, Mahogany."

"Well, fuck wit me then." We both laughed and he pulled the sheets from both of our heads.

"You want me to whip you up something for breakfast?" He asked, getting out of bed. I admired his physique as he stood before me shirtless and in a pair of basketball shorts similar to mine but in a different color.

"Yes. I'd love that. Let me check in on my daughter, real quick."

"Aight. There's a toothbrush and toothpaste in here for you, too."

"Okay, thank you."

I went to grab my phone from my bag, and it rang. Smiling, thinking it was Beautii calling to check in on me, I noticed Mo's number instead.

"I know, I know, I didn't text when I got to my destination," I said once the call connected.

"She *gone*, Hogany. She's fucking gone!" Her cries were silent but the heaviness in her voice held were audible.

"Who's gone, Mo?"

"Paris. We found her. Somebody...somebody killed my baby, Hogany. Why they do her like this, Mahogany? She ain't have nothing to do with nothing." I heard her heart and couldn't even find the words to comfort my friend. My line beeped with an incoming call from my mother, and I declined it. She called right back, letting me know I needed to answer.

"Hold on, Mo, please don't hang up." Clicking over, I spoke. **"Ma, I got an emer—."**

"Drop whatever you doing *right now* and get home!"

"Dad?" I asked, pulling the phone from my ear and checking to make sure it was my mother's name on the caller id.

"Somebody snatched up Beautii."

To Be Continued...

Charge It To The Game 3

Coming Soon

"Somebody snatched up Beautii."

Did you enjoy the read?
Let us know how much by leaving us a review on Amazon and
Goodreads.

Keep reading for a sneak peek of...

Charge It To The Game 3

Chapter One

MAHOGANY

Hearing my father's voice on the other end of the phone was a shock in itself but hearing that my baby had been snatched up stunned me into silence. I couldn't respond verbally. Instead, I ended the call, completely disregarding Mo on the other line. Nothing else mattered in this present moment. The fact that someone was bold enough to snatch my fucking kid up let me know that the threat was still among us and about to pull out the worst in me. From this moment forward, I knew I would no longer operate from the mindset of head of The Table. Mahogany the boss was treacherous, but Mahogany the mother was a motherfucka that would haunt your dreams and wake the dead behind my kid.

Grabbing my gun from underneath the pillow I'd slept on, I quickly traded Justice's basketball shorts for my jeans. Sliding my feet in my shoes, I snatched up my purse from the ottoman in front of his bed and made my way to his bedroom door without so much as a peep.

"Damn, Mama, you just gon' leave without saying bye or hittin' your mouth with some toothpaste?" I heard him say in a playful manner from behind me just as I was a few steps from his door.

I wasn't in a joking mood at all. Not giving myself a second to fully think my next move through, I spun around with my gun raised directly at his head. "Did you lure me here last night and have my kid snatched up?" Taking the gun off safety, silence fell over the room. My eyes turned to slits, and the look of lust I once had was now replaced with deadly fire.

With his eyes never leaving mine, Justice titled his head as if he were examining the gun to see if it was loaded.

"I don't have your kid, Mahogany. I hate to hear that she's even missing." His tone was even, but the anger and offense was there. The crease in his forehead gave it away as well. "While you're standing here having a stare down with me, you should be kicking down doors to find your little one."

"Excuse me?" Now, I was offended and didn't appreciate the condescending tone. My finger rested on the trigger, ready to squeeze.

"Mahogany, if you actually believed that I orchestrated or personally carried out that foul ass shit you just accused me of, you would've squeezed until the clip was empty. So, like I said, instead of having this face off with me, you should be kicking down doors and narrowing down your suspect pool."

My phone rang, and there was a knock at his door at the same time.

"Come in, Ma," he called out, his eyes never leaving mine.

"Hey, I was just... I know damn well..." Her voice trailed off, and I heard the sound of a gun cocking behind me. I wasn't the least bit fazed though. We could have a shootout in this bitch for all I cared. "Now, sweetheart, I'm not sure how you think this is gonna play out, but that young man you're standing in front of is my pride and joy. My heart in human form. From the day he was born, I promised his father that I'd be judged by twelve before I let him be carried by six. I'm sure you catch my drift."

"She's good, Ma." Justice spoke on my behalf. "Put y'all guns down and let me get dressed." He turned, walking away, leaving the two of us standing in the middle of his bedroom.

"I don't have time for this shit. I gotta go find my baby." Just saying the words out loud, my chest tightened, and air felt constricted. About facing, I was face-to-face with his mother.

She was a beautiful, middle-aged woman with rich, caramel colored skin like Justice. Her hair was pulled back from her face in a low ponytail, fully displaying the *fuck around and find out* look she had. I hadn't seen her last night when I arrived, and this wasn't the best introduction for the two of us.

"That ain't no way to show a man you like him, boo. I'm sure Antoinette taught you that. And I know she ain't snag a man of Coolie's stature by being so aggressive."

I didn't bother asking how she knew my mother, nor did I respond to her admiration for my dad. I'd wasted enough time. I needed to locate my child. I went to walk past her, and she put her hand on my arm, stopping me. Glancing down at her hand and back up at her face, she seemed unfazed by my stance.

"I don't know what's going on, but if you need anything, let us know. Me and your parents go way back." After one final look, she let my arm go, and I proceeded to make my exit.

Jumping in my car, I threw my purse in the backseat and sat my gun and phone in my lap. Leaning forward and resting my head on the steering wheel, my heart raced, and all of my emotions came pouring out of me. Hitting the steering wheel a few times, I let out a scream so loud I was sure it could be heard outside of the car. Somebody had my innocent child, and the thought of bodily harm being done to her made the hairs on my neck stand up. I knew I had to shake the emotions; my baby couldn't get my best efforts if I was out moving reckless.

One thing I knew for sure, I was at any and everyone's head until my daughter was back home safe and sound. Everyone's safety was in jeopardy at this point. Inhaling deeply, a full exhale followed as I started my car. Connecting my phone to Bluetooth, I made the command to call Briscoe. Unlike the recent times when I called him, he answered on the first ring.

"What I do now?"

"Meet me at my house. Somebody snatched up Beautii."

"Somebody did what?! What the fuck is you sayin' to me right now, Mahogany?"

"Look, I know just about as much as you right now, Briscoe, which is much of nothing. Just go to my house please. I'm on my way there, so I can figure this shit out."

"You mean so we can figure this shit out. This our mother-fuckin' child you talkin' bout, Hogany. What the fuck, man?!"

"You know what I mean, Briscoe. I ain't got time or fuckin' energy to go back-and-forth witchu about what I'm gon' do or what we gon' do. Let's just DO THIS SHIT, SO WE CAN GET OUR CHILD HOME!" I hit the end button on my steering wheel and shifted the car into drive.

Just as I went to drive off, two knocks at my window halted my push on the gas. Justice stood outside of my car with a facial expression I couldn't read and didn't have time to decode. I opened my mouth to tell him to back up, but before I could, he opened the passenger side door and slid into the seat.

"Time is not on our side. We'll hash that lil' shit out that happened inside at a later date once we find your little one. Just know that it'll be the last time you pull a gun out on me. Drive, Mahogany."

I didn't have it in me to have a war of words with him. Putting my foot on the gas, I mashed out. I was gonna find my child, and when I did, the person who'd taken her, or even had a hand in it, was going to die a slow and painful death that was sure to be whispered about for years.

"What did your daughter have on this morning?" Justice inquired, disturbing the silence I so desperately needed in order to focus and maintain a level head.

"I couldn't tell you. I was too busy laid up witchu when I should've been home being a mother."

"Aye, don't start that *woe is me* shit. That ain't gon' help get her back no faster. You need to continue to be that same boss you've been since the day I met you at my car wash. That's what's going to guarantee your daughter's safe return. When you get to acting on emotions is when shit goes left."

Tears pricked my eyes as he spoke, but I couldn't let them fall. Not because I didn't want to appear weak in front of him, but because tears weren't gonna do anything but piss me off further. I heard everything he said, but I was still overwhelmed with emotions. Being a mother made you both strong and weak at the same time — strong in that God saw fit to place a little human in your care that you'd move Heaven and Earth for and take on any hardship life had to offer just to keep them safe and weak in that parenting made you vulnerable and sometimes caused you to make erratic decisions based on emotions.

It was a tough role yet rewarding at the same time. Still, no matter how I felt at the moment, I knew for shit sure that nobody would sleep until I found Beautii. Just as I turned my car onto my street, my phone rang. An unknown number flashed on the car's dashboard. Disconnecting the phone from the Bluetooth, I picked it up. I stared at the screen and mentally prepared myself for bullshit. Taking in a deep breath and exhaling slowly, I let the call ring three times before swiping to answer and putting the phone to my ear.

"Hello?"

"Is this Mahogany?" the unknown caller spoke. I couldn't place the male voice, but it was clear he knew me.

"Who is this?" Parking right outside of my house, I kept the ignition running. The caller paused, and I could hear light breathing on the other end of the phone. **"Hello,"** I spoke again, my voice laced with irritation.

"Is this Mahogany?" the caller repeated.

"No, this isn't Mahogany. This is a bitch with little, no scratch that, no patience for this prank call bullshit. Now, you only have seconds to state your business or clear my motherfuckin' line." I'd put so much emphasis on the cuss words, spit flew from my mouth.

Justice tapped my shoulder and held up his phone for me to see. On the screen was his notes app. He typed for me to calm down and put the call on speakerphone. I did, and he kept his phone up next to mine. I could hear shuffling in the background, followed by what sounded like a door being opened.

"Get off me!" Hearing Beautii's voice clear as day, my body went still, and the phone slipped out of my hand, falling in my lap.

Without a second thought, Justice grabbed it and held it up to his mouth. **"How much?"** he asked the caller, taking control.

"Who da fuck is this?"

"That's not important. Give us a number." He was calm and calculating as he spoke.

"**Man, put the woman in charge back on the phone,**" the caller spat.

"**I'm here,**" I spoke through gritted teeth.

"**Good. As you can see, I have something of yours. The last thing I wanna do is hurt your little girl. I actually like kids. I want some of my own someday. I...**"

"**Whatever it is you want, you got it,**" I cut him off. "**Just let me speak to her.**"

"**Oh, my bad. She can hear you.**"

"**I'm here, Mommy. Please, please come get me.**"

I held my hand up to my mouth and bit my finger to contain my anger. "**Beautii, what I always tell you?**"

"**Anything or anyone that tries to come between us will be met with grave consequences.**"

"**That's right, my girl. Mommy coming. Believe that.**"

"**Alright, Colombiana,**" the male voice returned. "**I need 50K. I'll hit you with the details shortly.**" The line went dead.

"Motherfucka!" I screamed out. "I swear I'm gonna kill everybody involved. This bitch ass nigga kidnapped my kid for a measly 50K!" Not only was I seething mad, but I was offended. Fifty thousand dollars didn't even cover the jewelry in Beautii's jewelry box. "Okay, I see how we doing this. Y'all got the right one."

Also By Nai

Wrapped Up In A Hitta's Love For Christmas

Yours For The Taking

Seizing A Gangsta's Heart For The Summer

Thug Me The Right Way

Thug Me The Right Way 2

Thug Me The Right Way 3

A Summer To Remember With My Hitta

Snatched Up By A Hitta

Wet Dreams On Lockdown: The Unit Manager

Santa Sent Me A Real One For Christmas

Bossin' Up On The Plug

Bossin' Up On The Plug 2

In The Trenches With My Hitta

n The Trenches With My Hitta 2

Stealing A Queenpin's Heart

Stealing A Queenpin's Heart 2

A Piece of A Hustler's Heart

A Piece of A Hustler's Heart 2

A Thug's Love Mended My Heart

A Thug's Love Mended My Heart 2

A Summer To Remember With My New York Bae

A Summer Fling In New York

His Hood Love Gave Me Life

His Hood Love Gave Me Life 2

My Thug, My Sanctuary

Thug Kisses For Christmas

For The Love Of My Savage

Charge It To The Game

Other Books By
URBAN AINT DEAD

Tales 4rm Da Dale

The Hottest Summer Ever

Hittin' Licks For The Holidays: Atlanta

Wet Dreams On Lockdown: The Nurse

How To Publish A Book From Prison

By **Elijah R. Freeman**

Despite The Odds

By **Juhnell Morgan**

Good Girls Gone Rogue

Good Girls Gone Rogue 2

By **Manny Black**

Hittaz

Hittaz 2

Hittaz 3

Hittaz 4

Hittaz 5

Hittaz 6

Coldhearted

Coldhearted 2

Coldhearted 3

By **Lou Garden Price, Sr.**

Charge It To The Game

A Summer To Remember With My Hitta
Snatched Up By A Hitta
Santa Sent Me A Real One For Christmas
Wet Dreams On Lockdown: The Unit Manager
Thug Me The Right Way 2
Thug Me The Right Way 3
Seizing A Gangsta's Heart For The Summer
Yours For The Taking
Wrapped Up In A Hitta's Love For Christmas
By **Nai**

A Set Up For Revenge
A Set Up For Revenge 2
Wet Dreams On Lockdown: The Librarian
By **Ashley Williams**

Trickin' On A Heaux For Christmas
Homie Hoppin' For The Holidays
Wet Dreams On Lockdown: The Female C.O
Letters Of His Love
By **Telia Teanna**

The State's Witness
The State's Witness 2
The State's Witness 3
This Time Won't You Save Me
This Time Won't You Save Me 2
His Summer Side Piece
A Holiday Heist
By **Kyiris Ashley**

Stuck In The Trenches

Stuck In The Trenches 2

By **Huff Tha Great**

Melted The Heart Of A Menace

Wet Dreams On Lockdown: Lieutenant Grace

By **P. Wise**

Merry Trapmas

By **Mia Sky**

Thug Me The Right Way

By **DiamondATL & Nai**

Wet Dreams On Lockdown: The Counselor

By **Paris Iman**

Wet Dreams On Lockdown: The Male C.O

By **Tamyra Griffin**

Wet Dreams On Lockdown: The Captain

By **TN Jones**

Wet Dreams On Lockdown: The Warden

By **Shawnice**

Atlantastan

Atlantastan 2

By **Chris Green**

IN The Streetz

IN The Streetz 2

IN The Streetz 3

IN The Streetz 4
By **Tron Hill**

Hittin' Licks For The Holidays: New York
By **Freshh Moneyy**

Coming Soon From
URBAN AINT DEAD

The Hottest Summer Ever 2
THE G-CODE
Tales 4rm Da Dale 2
How To Invest In The Stock Market From Prison
By **Elijah R. Freeman**

Good Girls Gone Rogue 3
By **Manny Black**

Despite The Odds 2
By **Juhnell Morgan**

Charge It To The Game 3
By **Nai**

This Time Won't You Save Me 3
Healing The Heart Of A Detroit Gangsta
By **Kyiris Ashley**

Atlantastan 3
By **Chris Green**

IN The Streetz 5
By **Tron Hill**